T0132484

THE DARK SIDE
OF THE EARTH

Timothy A. Bramlett

authorHOUSE®

AuthorHouse™
1663 Liberty Drive
Bloomington, IN 47403
www.authorhouse.com
Phone: 1 (800) 839-8640

Published by AuthorHouse 01/03/2019

ISBN: 978-1-5462-5310-5 (sc)
ISBN: 978-1-5462-5308-2 (hc)
ISBN: 978-1-5462-5309-9 (e)

Library of Congress Control Number: 2019900124

Print information available on the last page.

This book is printed on acid-free paper.

Contents

Preface

I hope you enjoy this collection of unusual short stories that have evolved from a variety of sources, including dreams that I had and that demented mind of yours truly. You have to experience these for yourselves and draw your own conclusions. You might even learn something about yourself and others.

"The Dog That Went to College" is a story that evolved from my great love of man's best friend. Taking shape as a canine prodigy and ending up as a co-ed in a college. How bizarre is that? What happens when you combine a superb intellect with that of a devoted dog with a loving family? Is there a correlation between intelligence and devotion or are they separate entities?

"The 5th Street Church Café" came from a dream that I had that took shape with the idea that a church should be fun to go to instead of a habit that we practice every week. One thing I noticed while going to my Sunday morning ritual was that everybody seemed to be in a habit of doing everything the same way every week. People park in the same parking spot, enter the church through the same door, sit in the same seat in the same pew, and exit through the same door, every week. All done with relatively precise timing. A friend of mine hung his hat on the same peg every Sunday morning and picked it up on his way out. One Sunday morning I decided to put his hat on a different peg to see what happened. I noticed that he just picked up his hat and left as if nothing unusual had happened. Have we gotten so automated that we don't even notice changes? Are things really as they appear to be?

"The Other Half" came from another dream I had about a man who suddenly fell into a fortune, or so it seemed. He was, by definition, an ordinary Joe and didn't understand the workings of the upper crust of society. How was he going to handle the change? He was someone who drank Budweiser and ate saltine crackers with Vienna sausages. He loved canned spaghetti and potato chips. He drove a Chevy and lived in a modest house. He might just find this a bit too much or he might learn to love it. Then things changed. What then? Was it better or worse?

"The Junkyard Café" was from another dream. We're used to eating in conventional restaurants with all the amenities of what we're used to. Whoever thought of putting a restaurant in the middle of a junk yard? And what will happen with the health department? Surely, they will never approve of such a crazy idea. And what will the neighbors think? Or the rats? Or the groundhogs?

"The Dead Don't Die Sometimes" is a story about a man who "died," or did he? The age old question of what happens after death is explored in this story. When is a person really dead? Everyone wants to know and will leave no head stone unturned to find out, even if it's a cadaver in the autopsy room. Are you dying to find out what happens?

"The Evil Old Man" is the story about a man that everyone in in the neighborhood hates. Maybe hate is too harsh a word. Let's be a bit more charitable. I guess they just don't care much for him. He seems to be a crummy, selfish neighbor. But is he really like that or is all that rotteness just a façade to protect himself from some insecurity. Do people really change for the better or do they stay rotten to the end. You shall find out by reading this story. Maybe we should take a different look at people like that.

"The Island" is a tale about ordinary people that get put in unusual situations. Is it natural for a person to suspect that he or she is going to be murdered? How do you deal with such feelings? Being stuck on an island is bad enough but when you suspect that there is a murderer there is reason to be suspicious, or is it? Especially when there is nowhere to hide. It may not be exactly like Gilligan's Island but we'll see what happens without the professor to straighten things out.

"A Dry Day in Vance" is in a typical southwestern desert town that lacks something vital-rain. What are you going to do when you are miles away from the nearest river and days away by horse and wagon? Your water supply is dwindling. Are you going to hire a rain maker even though you don't believer in such nonsense? Desperate times call for desperate measures. There are flimflammers that are ready to take your money and run.

"The Snows of Pine Mountain" is the story about a group of people who crash their airplane in the middle of nowhere in a snow storm. How could anything be worse than that? What will happen to the only survivor of that crash? With my luck, I would be rescued by a desperate criminal. But even desperate criminals might have a side to them that we may have never seen.

"The Curse of Angelo" is a story about a couple of washed up city people, one a gangster and the other a private detective. They somehow end up together in the same jail cell. What then? They've been trying to kill each other for years. Are they even going to survive being in jail together. When they get out, do they help each other or do they go back the way they were?

"Sharkey And the Blips" is taken from some of my earlier stories about Sharkey and the Space Pirates, the Blips, and Thomas and Mary Caroline. The Blips are tiny human like creatures that live under ground. Somehow, Sharkey and his crew get involved with Thomas and Mary Caroline in a quest to help save the Blips from the wrath of modern times. How do you stop plans for a shopping center? Can the Blips be saved from the wrath of a bulldozer and something called "progress," or will they be swept under like a burrow of moles? You have to find out.

The final installment is a true story. In the summer of 1960, I spent a week at Camp Daniel Boone in western North Carolina when I was in the boy scouts. I was eleven years old at the time and it was a very interesting experience.

The Dog That Went to College

Let's make it clear from the start. Butch was no ordinary dog. You might even say he was a dog prodigy. Extremely intelligent and some may even say he was smarter than most of the people in the neighborhood. His little black nose seemed to be into everything, even from the start. He was furry, not short haired like a lab, and had the distinct look of a terrier mix. He was never self-conscious about his mixed breed background and it was never confirmed who the father was, but it was strongly suspected that the culprit was a friendly mutt rounder-about-town named Harvey. Butch's mom, Helga, was a sweetheart of a dog and loved by all the neighborhood kids. She lived up the street with her adopted family, the Smiths. They were two doors up from Mr. John Randle, his wife Gladys and their two children, Hal and Janet. The Randles lived at 275 Maple Street. They were promised one of Helga's pups, which they looked forward to adopting.

When it became well known that Helga was in the family way, it was an exciting time in the west end of the neighborhood. As the glorious moment drew near, the neighbors came to witness the blessed event. They brought puppy food, chew toys, pull ropes, baby beds and blankets, and other things that were obviously for larger puppies.

Butch was the boss of the litter from the start. He was an obvious alpha dog and never let the others doubt for a minute that he was in charge. Mother Helga had to put Butch in his place several times when he got a little too rough with his brothers and sisters.

In about six months, the Randles adopted one of the pups and named him "Butch." They waited until he was weaned from his mother before taking him home, at which time his own bed and bowl were waiting as well as free run of the house.

Butch grew fast and in no time at all, he was tugging and pulling and tumbling. His little sharp baby teeth were soon cutting happily into the unsuspecting flesh of an unwary human hand that carelessly ventured toward his friendly little furry mouth.

When Butch was almost a year old, it became obvious that he was no ordinary dog. He learned fast, much faster than the others in his litter. He was even making up games on his own. He was tricking the family out of food and treats at every opportunity. His demeanor was one of a trickster but one with a seemingly sense of humor. He often appeared to be in deep thought as he pondered his next move.

An event that seemed to set in motion a series of incredible events took place on a cool March Tuesday evening. Hal, the eldest child in the family, was playing a game of chess one day with his younger sister, Janet. Butch would watch intently, and he seemed to learn what each piece did. He noticed that the pawns moved forward, the bishops went diagonally, and the rooks moved straight ahead, backward, or straight left or right. By observing this, he learned what moves to make. He would nudge a pawn or a rook in the direction he thought was best and it turned out he was right most of the time. "Remarkable," Hal would say to his mom and dad. "This dog knows how to play chess."

"Impossible," his dad would say. "He's just a dog." Butch would look at him with indignation and a sense of pity that the father was so naive. A quick demonstration proved Hal to be right.

But Butch was much more than a chess player. He learned the alphabet and could actually read. He understood words and associated them with pictures. Soon, he was playing scrabble, spelling out words with his paws with a special alphabet devised by the father, who by this time was convinced that Butch must be a canine genius.

When the neighborhood kids came over to witness this incredible display of intellect, they would make up games, which Butch quickly learned.

Soon, word got to the local television and newspaper. An article was written about how Butch was a "genius" among the canine community. The TV station did a special program on Butch, featuring him in a question and answer session. He was given words and seemed to match them with pictures. Everyone was amazed that he had actually learned the alphabet and was able to form words and recognize them. He seemed to have a photographic memory.

But Butch's big break came when the local chess champion, Horace Kripes, challenged him to a chess game in the television studio. With the help of Hal and Janet moving the pieces, Butch would nudge the chess piece and then touch the proper square with his nose. The kids would move the piece. Kripes was defeated in twelve moves. "Incredible," the media reported. "It's got to be a trick," they would say. But it was no trick. Butch was for real.

The headlines the next day read, "Butch Randle is a chess master" as they showed his picture on the front page with his paws on the chessboard.

And, of course, the inevitable happened. He was given an I.Q. test by the local high school faculty. He scored an astounding 130. Of course they had to provide the proper way for Butch to answer the questions but to everyone's surprise, he was the smartest "person" in the entire school. And just to prove it was no fluke, he was given another test and he scored even higher, a 135.

As time went on, Butch became more of a celebrity. He cruised through puppy hood and his baby teeth were replaced by his permanent teeth, and his soft puppy fur was replaced by the coarser, more wiry, adult hair. He learned more and more things. He was able to accomplish more important feats that astounded more and more people.

"I think it's time for bigger and better things for Butch," Mr. Randle said one day to the family. "What did you have in mind?" Gladys asked.

"At work today I was approached by dean Alvin McAllister from Hartley College." They think we can make a lot of money with Butch."

What are you talking about," Gladys asked candidly.

"I mean he thinks Butch can go to college." Mrs. Randle almost fell over in her chair and the children were dumbfounded. Butch go to college? How absurd is that, they inquired.

The next day, they all went to the Hartley College registrar to discuss this bizarre possibility. After a lengthy discussion with dean McAllister and the registrar, it was decided that even if it didn't work out, it was some positive publicity that the college needed.

"Enrollment is down somewhat," the Dean stated as he sat up in his chair. "Butch could be the shot in the arm we need to bring more people in.'

"But, keep in mind," the registrar added. "He must take the SAT," If he scores high enough, I can recommend to the board that Butch be accepted. Besides, freshman Butch Randle might even get a scholarship."

It all seemed sort of crazy. Whoever heard of a dog going to college? "What's in it for us?" Mr. Randle asked. "After all, Butch will be leaving home and the children won't like this very much."

"Monetary compensation," the Dean answered succinctly. "We'll pay you a goodly amount of money to let us put your dog through four years of college. As far as the amount, I'd have to discuss this with the board of directors."

Mr. and Mrs. Randle decided to talk this over with the kids before he proceeded any farther with the project. After all, they all needed the money, regardless of how much it would be.

The children were, as expected, upset over this. But, after realizing that they could see him on weekends and get some money out of the deal, they reluctantly agreed. Dollar signs do have a lot of influence and Butch was halfway to the halls of ivy.

And Butch jumped through the hoops with flying colors. On the SAT, he scored 1,800 and was in the 90th percentile. This meant he was in the top 10%. He passed the physical given to him by their local veterinarian.

A special meeting was held with the administrative staff at Hartley and after many hours of debate, it was decided to give it a try. There were many logistical problems to overcome such as housing, special food, training a person to take care of Butch. But, in time, it was all worked out. In fact, half of his tuition was paid for as well as all of his food. It looked like a good deal for all concerned.

During the summer before classes started, a senior was chosen, someone who had already been accepted to a veterinarian school, who they had picked to take care of Butch and some of the unique problems that would arise. His name was Tom Wilson and he and Butch got acquainted during a session at Hartley. They got along exceptionally well and were assigned to Butler Dorm, room 426. Butch had his own bed, of course, and a special diet that was provided by the college.

As the big day arrived in September, Hal and Janet were in tears, having to say goodbye to their good friend Butch. The first check was already received by the Randles and it helped ease the pain for the family. Butch was excited and seemed to look forward to his new adventure. He was a celebrity now with a bright future and he seemed to know it. He had a bit of a swagger in his walk and his tail wagged with more authority and confidence than ever. The look in his eyes revealed a bit of a pretentious arrogance.

"It's only going to be for four years," John said to his family. Then we'll have Butch back again right here at home."

"Only," Janet stated as she lowered her head.

"And what if he wants to go to grad school?" Hal asked. "What am I saying? It's not like he will become a professor or anything."

On that cool fall day in September, the Randles arrived at Butler dorm and Tom was there to greet them. And not only was Tom there but the news media was blitzing the area with reporters. It was a big event. Butch seems to relish the moment, wagging his tail and looking smug. He was caught up in the excitement and hardly looked at his family. They stuck a microphone in Butch's face and he responded with a sarcastically sounding "woof."

"Goodbye Butch," Hal and Janet said to Butch as they fought back the tears. Butch glanced back at them, then turned around and headed for the door to the dorm and disappeared. Butch never looked back.

The Randles sadly went back home. "We're scheduled to see Butch next Saturday at 3:00 pm," John stated, hoping to fight back the depression of the moment. "I'm not sure he even cares if we come and see him. He seems to be having too much fun." The family was silent as they drove home and tried to accept the situation.

Meanwhile, Butch was having the time of his life. He was a real celebrity. Everyone in the dorm wanted to get a good look at Butch and to test his intelligence. To play him in a game of chess. To see if this was all real. Even touching his fur was a thrill to some of the students.

Tom was an ideal room mate and fixed Butch his dinner. Butch insisted on following Tom so it became apparent that he was obliged to take him to the cafeteria. He was, of course, greeted with lots of pets and Butch loved every minute of it. Soon, the ham scraps were heading his way along with other food morsels that the students were discarding.

"Doesn't he miss his family?" Barbara Jones said as she stroked his ears. "He doesn't seem to," Tom answered. "At least not now. I think he's too excited."

Butch had an interesting schedule of classes, which started the following Monday. First, it was Physical Education. Then a math class, followed by Spanish. In the afternoon, he had a history class followed by biology.

Butch sat attentively in classes, absorbing every word, seemingly immune from distractions. His specially designed testing procedure allowed Butch to move his nose to the multiple choices, which he would mark. His scores were remarkable. "He's doing very well," one professor stated. "His power of concentration is better than any of my students."

In Phys. Ed., he was the fastest runner and had more agility than all the other students. He sat a record in the 50 and 100 yard dash that would never be broken. He could do hurdles and relays like an Olympic star. and there was talk about him being on the track team.

As he followed Tom to the cafeteria, he developed a taste for "human" food and decided that his special "dog food" was just not his cup of tea any more. As Butch began putting on weight from morsels from some of the students, Tom began to get concerned and banned the students from feeding him.

This, however, did not apply to a party one night. Butch had been instructed to stay in his room while Tom socialized at the Zombie room-a special area for senior parties. Butch pushed the latch on the door and left his room, following Tom's scent till he arrived at the party. Letting himself in, he was, of course, warmly received as Tom failed to notice him at first. Butch found a glass of beer someone had left on an end table and proceeded to try it. 'Not bad,' Butch thought to himself as he finished it, followed by a burp. By the time Tom realized Butch was there, he was sitting the lap of a girl with another beer in his possession. 'The pretzels aren't bad, either,' Butch thought. Finally noticed by Tom, Butch had already become a bit tipsy. After all, he wasn't used to drinking beer. Tom escorted a slightly inebriated dog back to his room. By that time Butch had already been made an honorary member of the Hartley College drinking club. Suffering from a slight hangover the next morning, Butch decided to skip breakfast and sleep it off.

When news got back to dean McAllister, he expressed concern that Butch needed to be watched more closely.

"He seems to be manipulating us," Tom said. "He knows how to get his way."

"Well," answered McAllister, "make Butch walk the straight and narrow from now on. If word gets back to the Randles, they may take Butch out of Hartley. Enrollment is already up, maybe an all time high. I want to keep it going up."

In the dorm poker games, he teamed up with Tom. Quickly learning about poker, he would point to the cards with his nose for Tom to discard and was soon displaying an incredible ability to win. His keen sense of logic, along with his poker face seemed to make him into a great poker player. He even found out that if he wagged his tail, the opponents would think he had a winning hand, only to realize it was a trick. Once he was accused of cheating but an assertive growl and show of teeth put an end to any further accusations.

He became a member of the chess club and was defeating all competitors. Soon, he was the champion chess player of Hartley College. It was suggested that he travel to other colleges for demonstrations.

Meanwhile, the Randles made their weekly visit to Butch, only to find him preoccupied with the routine of college life. Once when they came to visit him, he had sneaked out of his dorm room and was away at the art studio, posing for a painting.

At the end of the first quarter grading period, Butch had made the Dean's list. The news media was swarming around campus. As the Randles arrived during their weekly visit, Butch was caught up in the excitement and didn't even notice his family. They left for home and had a rather sobering conference among the family when they got back.

"Well," Mr. Randle said with some consternation. "I think we've lost Butch."

"Sure seems that way," Gladys answered.

"He likes college life better than us," Hal added sadly as Janet began to sob.

"We might as well tell Dean McAllister to turn him over to Tom Wilson for keeps," Mr. Randle finally concluded. "Tomorrow, we'll go back to Hartley College and give them the news."

Meanwhile, back at the dorm on that very same evening, Butch sat in his bed and pondered his schedule for the next day. Tom tried to develop a routine so Butch would know what to expect.

"Here's a treat, Butch," Tom said as he reached his hand in a bag. Butch knew it was time for a snack and he smacked his lips. "You'll need a good night's sleep. Tomorrow you will be doing a swimming test. If you make it, you might get exempt from some of the phys. ed requirements."

Butch was a great swimmer. Not a fast swimmer but with good stamina. He was no retriever but when he was at home, he could get the ball that was thrown out in a lake and bring it back. Butch thought it was a bit boring but it seemed to please the family so he continued to do it as many times as they threw the ball. 'They were so easily amused,' he thought to himself.

As Tom turned off the light, Butch began to think about his family. He started thinking about John and Gladys but most of all, he missed the kids, Hal and Janet. He remembered chasing a ball in the back yard and climbing on the bed on a cold night. He thought about those cozy evenings when he would sit in front of the fireplace while the family watched television. He even thought about jumping into a cold lake and fetching that red rubber ball. It was a time where there were no schedules to keep, no learning words and phrases. No numbers to remember. Just an occasional chess game or a brisk walk through the park. He drifted off to sleep but it was a restless sleep. Then, and all too soon, the alarm clock went off. "Time to get up, old boy," Tom would say as he yawned and slid out of bed, his bare feet hitting the floor with a familiar thud.

'Tom was nice,' Butch thought, 'a good friend, kind and gentle,' but he just wasn't his family.

"How's the genius dog doing today?" Tom's friend Jack asked as they headed for the cafeteria. "Doing fine, Jack," he answered. "He's going to swimming class this morning.

"Have you taught him the backstroke yet?" Jack asked.

"No," Tom answered with a laugh. "The dog paddle is all he can do but he does it well. We're hoping he will get exempt from any more phys. ed."

Tom finished breakfast with Butch by his side. Then they exited the cafeteria and headed for the gymnasium. They passed by a parking lot where a family was greeting a student. They had their dog with them and he was really glad to see the girl. Butch took notice and he began to think about his family again. A certain melancholy sadness began to creep into Butch's mind. Maybe the real dog mentality was finally beginning to emerge. He didn't walk quite as fast as he usually did and Tom thought Butch might not be feeling well.

"You okay, boy?" he asked. Butch looked up at Tom with soulful eyes. Something Tom had not seen before. "Your nose is cold," Tom added. "A dip in the pool with make you feel better."

Butch did not know it, but his family was on their way to Hartley College for one final trip. Butch jumped in the water, swam a few a few laps around the pool, not with the enthusiasm that Tom had expected but, nevertheless, it was good enough to convince the instructor that Butch could swim very well. Tom lifted him out of the water, dried him off with a towel and Butch shook the rest of the loose water off his fur.

"That's fine," the instructor said. "Old Butch is qualified. He won't have to do Phys. Ed. 102." They headed back toward the dorm but Tom decided they would take a detour first. They just had enough time for a snack and a rest before biology class. "Maybe a little walk will perk you up," Tom said.

"Let's stop at the student center for a little snack," Tom stated as they hurried toward the building. "I didn't have enough breakfast."

As they entered the building, a car arrived at Butler Dorm. It was the Randles. They entered the dorm and asked the dorm advisor to see Butch and Tom.

"They're not here," he said politely. "I think they went to the gymnasium."

"There's no point in us seeing Butch," Mr. Randle said sadly to the advisor. "Just tell Tom Wilson that Butch is his dog now."

"Does Tom know this?" the advisor asked.

"No, but he will understand." Gladys and the kids were waiting in the car.

As Mr. Randle and the dorm advisor talked, a strange feeling came over Butch in the student center. It was like he knew his family was at the dorm. Suddenly, he jumped up and ran out the door and up the hill toward Butler Dorm. Tom was in hot pursuit. "Where are you going?" he yelled at Butch. "Come back."

And just as John Randle was heading for his car, Butch came bounding toward him.

"It's Butch!!" Janet said excitedly as she flew out of the car to greet their dog.

"He seems to be glad to see us," Hal added as he joined Janet.

After a face licking and a frantic tail wagging they had never seen before, Butch jumped in the car as the kids followed.

Just then Tom arrived out of breath from running. "I ran as fast as I could to catch him but he's awfully fast. He's a champion sprinter, you know."

"I think Butch is trying to tell us something," John Randle said. "I think he wants to come home."

"He really did miss us," Janet said. "I wonder what changed his mind?"

Butch would not get out of the car. He looked at Tom and held out his paw as if to shake hands and to thank him for his kindness and concern. "I'll miss you, ol' boy," Tom Wilson said sadly as he petted Butch on the head. "But I think you need to be with your family now."

Butch then turn his eyes on Hal and Janet. He never looked back at Hartley College as he rode home with the Randles. He was through with college life. He realized what he really wanted and missed. Something every dog really wants. A family and a home.

But Butch was missed greatly at Hartley. They did award him an honorary B.A. degree in Psychology. "He deserves a degree in psychology," dean McAllister said. "He sure used a lot of it on us."

Butch lived with the Randles from then on. He never wanted to leave again. He lived out the rest of his days as a normal, happy dog.

He curled up on the rug in front of the fireplace as the Randles watched television. He enjoyed chasing that silly rubber ball that they threw in the lake. And all the money in the world couldn't make the Randles send him away again. Butch got educated at Hartley college and found what out what life was all about. And so did the Randles.

5TH Street Church Cafe

It was another slow Sunday morning at the 5th Street Christian Church under an overcast sky. The temperature was in the low 70's. The minister, Joe Williams, stood up in the pulpit and gazed out across the meager gathering of faithful followers. The usual people were in their usual seats, wearing their usual faces, most seemingly unaware that church attendance had steadily dropped over the past year. 'No new faces,' Williams thought to himself as he stood up for the benediction and scanned the pews. The choir sang well but seemed to be rather sparse, too.

As preacher Williams spoke, he could hear an echo. The church sanctuary lacked the proper acoustics and the lack of people emphasized that fact, allowing a reverberation that reminded Williams of being on top of a mountain, yelling at the top of his lungs to the bears and other critters below.

As Williams glanced to the left rear of the sanctuary, he noticed something he'd never seen before. Somehow, he missed this when he looked around. A young man sat in the rear pew, dressed in a black suit and white shirt. 'A new face,' the preacher thought as he perked up somewhat. 'I hope this becomes a trend. That would be job security.'

As the service progressed, the mystery man sat quietly in the rear and sang hymns with the rest of the sparse congregation, prayed with the others, and was quiet and reverent. After the service was over he met with minister Williams.

The man was about five foot seven, weighed about 165 pounds, had piercing dark brown eyes. He had on what appeared to be an expensive suit with a diamond stud in the middle of his silk tie.

"Good morning, pastor," he said reverently reaching out his hand. "My name is Al Verona."

"Good morning to you," preacher Williams responded, shaking his hand. "It's always nice to see new faces."

"You don't know me," Verona stated, "but my family went to church here many years ago. A long time before you were here and I thought I'd attend for old time sake. Just to see what the old church looks like now."

"I put a check in the collection plate for $300."

"I'm speechless," Williams said. "It couldn't have come at a better time. Our donations have been way off and our light bill is due."

"Glad to help," Verona said. "I noticed that your attendance was really low. What seems to be the problem?"

"I wish I knew," the minister said. "I hope it's not me."

"You delivered a marvelous sermon," the man stated, managing a warm smile. "I have an idea that might get this church back on its feet, if you're interested in hearing it?"

"I'm open to any suggestions," Williams answered.

Al looked around to see if anyone was listening and said, "where can I meet you. I'll need to lay it out so you can take it to your board of directors, or whatever you call your governing body."

"What about tomorrow at the restaurant down the street, say about eight o'clock tomorrow morning. We'll have breakfast. My treat."

"I'll be there," Verona answered. He exited the church and got into a large expensive, black car and drove off.

At eight the next morning, Williams arrived at the restaurant and noticed the mystery man seated in a booth. He walked over and greeted him, "Good morning, Mr. Verona."

"Good morning, Mr. Williams," he answered. The preacher sat down in the booth opposite the man as he sipped on coffee.

"I'm glad you came, Mr. Williams. I have an idea you might be interested in. But first, would you like a cup of coffee?"

"Yes, thank you," was his response. The waitress brought the minister a cup and they proceeded to discuss the business at hand.

"Now," Williams stated cautiously, "what did you have in mind."

"Well," Verona answered as he took another sip of coffee, "you probably gathered already from the car I'm driving that I have a lot of money. I have made a fortune in the computer business. I had a life changing experience, which I'd rather not get into, but it made me realize how important it is to help others. I've been donating large amounts of money to charities."

Williams looked stunned. An opportunity like this is beyond belief. He was sure that Verona was going to offer to give the church a large donation.

"I have an idea that money is not the solution to the problem here," Verona reasoned. "I could donate to the church a large sum of money but it wouldn't bring in a lot of people. You can make the church four times bigger than it already is but if you don't have people to fill it, it's not worth much."

"That's very true," Williams agreed. "So, what did you have in mind?"

Just then, two plates of food arrived. The waitress presented the two men with a plate of pancakes, link sausages, and syrup. "I hate to discuss business on an empty stomach," Verona stated. "Dig in."

Williams enjoyed his breakfast and almost forgot what they were there for. They talked about the weather and the old minister that was there when Al Verona's parents were attending the 5th Street Christian Church.

"I remember hearing about preacher Thompkins," Williams said. "Did you ever attend here when he was preaching?"

"No, sir," Verona said as he took a sip of coffee. I was living with my aunt and uncle about fifty miles away. It was a broken home situation."

"I'm sorry," Williams said as he looked down.

"It's okay," Verona stated. "I had a good life with them. But I heard a lot about your church. A lot of good things. That's why I want to help out all I can."

"Any help would be greatly appreciated, I assure you of that," Williams concluded.

"Here's the plan," Verona said as he took out a pad and pen. "Have you ever heard of church cafes?"

"Never heard of that," Williams said with a great deal of interest.

"It takes a lot of money to do," Al stated, "but I have enough to do the job right. You see, it involves renovating your sanctuary and converting it into a restaurant."

"Well, I don't know about that," Williams said as he sat up straight in his chair. "It sounds pretty radical."

"It has happened in a number of churches that are floundering," Verona said. "In fact, I can show you some statistics that proves that it has saved a number of churches from going under."

"Interesting," Williams said with a bit of skepticism.

"I would, of course pay for the whole thing. Your sanctuary would have a restaurant, tables, the works. The congregation would sit in the booths and tables and watch the sermon and participate in the service just like they always did. The choir would be up there with you and do their thing. It would be exactly like it is now except the audience could eat, drink, and relax. I guarantee it would triple your attendance, maybe more. And donations always increase on a full stomach."

Williams thought a minute. "Well, I don't know. I'd have to present it to the board for approval and I'm not sure they would go for it."

"I'll present it to them," Verona said.

"It's a deal," Williams said. "I will call a special meeting for next Tuesday at 7 PM."

"I'll be there," Verona said as they shook hands. Then they left the restaurant.

Al Verona was at the church right on time with a briefcase and a plan. He, along with pastor Williams and the six member church board entered the fellowship hall and took their seats. They had been briefed about the meeting and immediately showed skepticism about this outrageous plan. But something happened to change their mind. It was a problem with the budget that seemed to put things in a different light.

Verona introduced himself and passed out information about his plan to turn the church around. He quoted statistics and showed pictures. He was asked why he was willing to do this.

"As I told pastor Williams, I am extremely wealthy. I can renovate and rebuild this church and never miss the money. I think of myself as a benevolent philanthropist, and humanitarian. I ask nothing in return but the satisfaction of knowing that I did something for my fellow man."

The board softened their stand and began to see the benefits of this endeavor. There were, of course, legalities, and it was assured by Mr. Verona that all was taken care of.

"He's a God send," one of the board members finally said. "I think our church will have a new life."

In a closed session, the board voted unanimously to accept Al

Verona's generous offer, with the understanding that all the money that was made from the cafe would go back into the church treasury.

Work began on the church project very quickly with Mr. Verona standing on the sidelines making sure everything was in order and to the satisfaction of the board and congregation. There were, of course, skeptics, that were not sure this was a good idea but as soon as the renovation started taking place, most of the skeptics were converts.

"I hired a construction crew that has done this type of work before," he said to pastor Williams as the workers began tearing down walls. "They know what they're doing." At first it looked like a tornado had hit their church but, gradually, it all began to take shape and was a thing of beauty.

And the work progressed magnificently. Not only did Verona's workers make a fantastic dining room out of the sanctuary, they also renovated the classrooms and fellowship hall. They added a special room for storage deep in the basement, only accessible by Verona and his workers. He explained to the pastor. "My workers have a lot of valuable equipment and they like for it to be locked up."

They painted the walls and put in new windows. They re-did the flooring and took care of all the permits and legal work. And all the time, Al Verona oversaw the workings and interacted with the minister and the board. It was a pleasure to watch and it took a lot less time than expected. The workers seemed to be focused on doing a good job and working fast. In a matter of a few months the project was finished and it was ready for the grand opening.

In a special service the following Sunday morning, pastor Williams said, before an unexpectedly large crowd, including the news media, that this was the beginning of a new era. All people were welcome to come to the 5th Street Christian Church. "Sit down," he would say. "Order some breakfast and have something to drink. Relax and enjoy the service."

The choir sang even better than before. The acoustics were improved and the music was beautiful and inspiring. The sermons were better than ever because reverend Williams was inspired by this metamorphosis. When word got around, the crowds increased every week. Soon, there was a need for reservations on Sunday morning. There was talk of adding another service and also one on Wednesday night. Waitresses were added and the tips went into the collection plate.

And one Sunday morning not long after the opening of the 5th Street Church Cafe, Mr. Verona stood up before the congregation and made an announcement. "My good friends, pastor, choir, and cafe personnel. It's time for me to leave and move onto other projects. I leave you with the knowledge that there is still good in the world. Some of my workers have decided to stay with your church and become members. They have volunteered to maintain the storage room and be in charge of maintenance on the whole church, free of charge." The congregation roared with approval. "You can be proud of your new church and it is my sincere hope that your sanctuary will be filled to capacity every Sunday from now on, like it is today. I bid you farewell and good luck."

The congregation gave Mr. Verona a standing ovation and he left.

"What a wonderful man," the pastor said as he was almost in tears.

Meanwhile, Al Verona went to a hotel room on the west end of town where he met with some of his friends. Among them were Louie LaRoche, Larry Gilmer, and Pat Hooligan.

"Well, we did it again. It's all set up. We have some of our people going to that church now. They're running the cafe and soon, we will be running our counterfeiting operation from the basement."

"Too bad we can't make some money off their Bingo games?" Big Louie asked with a smirk on his face.

"The Bingo games are another way for the church to make some extra money," Al answered. "We can't get involved with that."

"Yeah," Larry stated. "Churches are exempt from gambling laws."

Pat added. "Who would accuse a church of doing anything illegal."

Al stated, "We added a few new members to the church and while they are having fun with bingo, we're using the maintenance room for our real payoffs."

Al explained that under the 5th Street Christian Church they had just renovated, they had built a complex counterfeiting operation with contacts all over the area. It was there they would control their illegal activities, hidden from the police and FBI. Who would suspect something like that going on under a church? They all had a big laugh.

Meanwhile, the 5th Street Church Cafe was thriving. Every Sunday morning, their sanctuary was full. And later, those who couldn't get a seat were standing. The minister was preaching better than he ever was, the choir was singing like angels, and the cafe could hardly keep up with hamburgers, hot dogs, french fries, drinks, pies, and sandwiches. They were raking in the money, hand over fist and all in the name of the Lord.

"I didn't know church could be so much fun," one patron said as he and his family sat in a booth reading the church bulletin in one hand and a menu in the other. They watched and listened to the sermon while the waitress brought them their food.

Volunteers were coming out of the woodwork as the church was adding new members almost every week.

Meanwhile, Verona's men were working in the basement, the congregation oblivious to what was going on beneath the church. For every dollar they church was making on cafe proceeds and donations, the printing presses were producing a million dollars a week.

Unfortunately, the other churches in the neighborhood were getting the worst end of the deal. People were leaving their own church and heading for 5th Street. It was this animosity and suspicion that caused an inquiry as to the nature of the success of this once impoverished church.

"When the novelty wears off, they will return," one minister said to his congregation.

"Or," as a deacon said to a cross town minister, "we could get on the bandwagon ourselves."

The inquiry was turned over to the proper authorities and soon, the FBI, who had been tipped off by a member of another church, started an investigation.

It was on a rainy night in August that the inevitable raid took place. The FBI busted down the door to the basement revealing a myriad of computers, printing presses, and files. The church "maintenance crew" sat stunned at this turn of events. Records showed a vast network of illegal money that spanned the entire southeast United States.

As the smoke cleared and the whole gangster operation was revealed, the embarrassment was overwhelming to the congregation of the 5th Street Church Cafe. Al Verona and his "maintenance crew" were charged with counterfeiting.

"So," the minister said to the authorities, "All this was just a front for illegal activities."

"Right under your noses," the FBI agent said.

The church was allowed to keep their cafe but, as expected, the novelty never wore off. Some of the new members who had jumped ship from other churches began to wander back to the fold of their previous church.

The 5th Street Church Cafe continued to flourish with the curiosity seekers and people that decided to join the church, deciding that this was a lot better than sitting in an uncomfortable pew for an hour.

As pastor Williams was quoted as saying, "Although our success was cloaked in deceit and crime, you can't deny that our church was saved. The Lord works in mysterious ways."

THE OTHER HALF

Jeff Farley was a very lucky man. He had just turned 35 when he woke up one sunny morning and realized he was very wealthy. And it seemed to happen so suddenly. An ordinary man with an ordinary job but was abruptly thrust into the nouveau riche echelon. How did this happen? Simple. He inherited a fortune.

Jeff had a college education and had worked in a variety of jobs. He had been a teacher's aide, a lab technician at a hospital, a clerk, and when times really got tight, he had to settle for bag boy at a local supermarket. He was also a bricklayer helper, a janitor, and worked at a car wash. He had to take what he could get. There were not many jobs available for a man with his college degree.

Jeff had been engaged to be married but his fiancé Beverly saw no future with him and even said he was "lazy." Her parents even stated that he "would bring nothing to the marriage." A more affluent beau came along and Beverly dropped Jeff like a hot potato. On his own with a broken heart, he found that he was at his lowest point.

But, that all changed one day when he was called in for the reading of a will from a very wealthy uncle who lived two thousand miles away. He never really knew uncle Bud but had heard how well off he had been. It was a big surprise when he was called into a lawyer's office that bright sunny day in March.

Uncle Bud was not noted for his generosity and was a bit of a jerk. Everyone knew this and when he became wealthy from the ground up, he thought everyone else should be able to do the same. Bank president, stock broker, it all added up to one thing, wealth, and lots of it.

Jeff figured that if dear old uncle Bud left him anything at all, and that was a million to one long shot against, it would be a copy of "How to get Rich" or maybe a book entitled. "You're Going to be a Bum All Your Life."

But maybe his new found wealth from old Bud might have been because Jeff never bothered him or asked for anything. On the rare occasions that Jeff saw his uncle, they seemed to get along very well. There was a certain sparkle in Bud's eye when Jeff was around. And although uncle Bud never had any children of his own, maybe Jeff was his imaginary adopted son. This proved that he must have felt something for his good-for-nothing nephew. A chemistry that was unexplainable. Maybe in different circumstances they might have even been golf buddies. Or maybe gone on fishing trips together. But Bud was much too busy running his businesses to have time for trivial relationships.

So, the whole family was stunned beyond belief when the will was read and everything was left to Jeff. A lot of animosity settled in and the whole clan was bewildered. Needless to say, there was stiff opposition to this "travesty of justice" and lawsuits would ensue. Contesting the will would prove fruitless to the group and they felt they deserved the fortune.

But when the dust settled, Jeff was the winner and loser. He won a fortune but due to the nasty court trial, he lost the friendship with all the close relatives he had. Or, maybe their friendships were just skin deep after all. "Surely Jeff would share his wealth with us," they would say amongst themselves.

For Jeff, who had originally planned on sharing this bounty with his relatives, had a change of heart after all the harsh words toward him were said and the lawsuit brought out the stark reality of what his family really thought about him.

"I guess water must be thicker than blood," he said to himself.

For Jeff, it was an opportunity beyond belief. He moved out of town and thoughts of Beverly gradually faded into his distant past.

Jeff moved to the ritzy part of a nearby city and bought a house in Hawthorne Heights on Queen Haven Avenue. It was a gigantic house. Three stories, a wrap around porch with lots of large oak trees shading almost the whole house. The ceilings were high and the rooms were huge. It had six bed rooms, four bathrooms, and two kitchens. There was a large fireplace in the living room with crystal chandelier. He's never even been in a house like this before, let along owned one. And, best of all, it was fully furnished. Chairs and sofas, paintings on the wall, and carpeting on the floor.

"Wow," he said out loud and noticed a distinct echo. "It sounds like an auditorium."

Soon, his real estate agent Mr. Wasser came by to welcome him to the neighborhood and have a couple of documents signed. "Welcome, Mr. Wasser," Jeff said as he came through the thick oak doors. They shook hands.

"Boy, you've got it made," Mr. Wasser said as he scanned the living room, looking up, down, and side to side. "You realize you have one of the best houses in the city, don't you."

"That's what they say," Jeff said sheepishly. "It might be a bit too much house for me."

"Nonsense," Mr. Wasser stated. "You'll have this house filled up in no time. Ever think about a butler and a maid?"

"Well, not really," Jeff added. "Think I need all that?"

"Well, sure. You can't take care of this place all by yourself. You'll need a gardener, too. I can arrange all that for you."

"I'll have to think about that," Jeff asserted.

"And one other thing, my boy," Mr. Wasser said as he put his hand on Jeff's shoulder. "You really ought to get rid of that jalopy parked out front and get you a rich person's car."

"Yeah, I guess I need to do that."

"Have you seen the basement?" Wasser asked.

"Yes, it's a fully stocked wine cellar with a recreation room. The works."

Mr. Wasser left with some names and phone numbers for maids, butlers, and gardeners. It all had not yet sunk in and Jeff still was overwhelmed by it all.

He wandered over to the bay windows on the south side and peered out. There was another house beside his that was just about as big. He looked up and it was also a three story mansion. Then, something caught his eye. On the second floor, a woman was looking down as him through a large open window. She smiled and waved. Jeff instinctively waved back and then she disappeared.

'I wonder who that was,' he muttered to himself.

A few minutes later, he heard a knock on the front door. "Oh boy, my first visitor," he said to himself, already feeling a bit lonely.

Answering the door, it happened to be the woman he saw in the house next door. He recognized her blue shirt and blonde hair.

"Hi," she said with a smile. "I'm Doris. I noticed you moved in and I just wanted to welcome you to the neighborhood."

"Thanks," Jeff said sheepishly as he introduced himself. "Won't you come in."

Doris came inside and started looking around. "Wow," she said. "You must be rich."

"I'm doing all right," Jeff answered with a smile.

"Well, I'm doing fine, too," she said. "My dad set me up pretty well.

He owns McAllister Enterprises. Do you live alone?"

"Why yes," Jeff said. "Do you?"

"I sure do. But I have lots of friends who drop by. It's sort of like a club. We hang out together. Hey, we're having a party tonight and I'd like for you to come."

Jeff agreed and was ready for his first high class encounter with other rich folks.

That evening he came to the party and was welcomed by a host of people. Some old, some young, some middle aged. It was a fancy party, all right. Exactly what he expected. Caviar, expensive wine, classical music in the background. Expensive clothes and shoes. Jewelry that would sparkle clean across the room. Cars parked outside that were ultra expensive.

"How are you, my boy?" and elderly gentleman said as he held out his hand. "How are your stocks and bonds?"

Jeff answered, "great, sir."

Suddenly, Doris wandered over and welcomed him. "Great to see you, Jeff," she stated with a martini in her hand. "I want you to meet some other people." He wandered around meeting all kinds of people. Women with large pearls and diamonds. Men with Rolex watches and large rings. Food that he'd never seen before and lots of odd shaped forks and spoons. Some large and some small. But all sparkling majestically in the light. It had been a heck of a night.

Jeff was finally ready to leave the party. He said goodbye to his host after made lots of friends. They were all very nice to him. He suddenly realized that they wanted nothing from him except friendship, small talk, and a chance to exchange ideas. No requests for money or anything else. Just a genuine desire to have him as their friend and be part of their circle of friends. He was even invited to play golf at the city's private country club and to become a member. Jeff had been accepted one hundred percent.

Jeff had finally found his niche, he thought. As he retired for the night, a warm feeling came over him. He tucked himself into bed, gazed outside at the glowing streetlight that produced a yellowish glow in his bedroom. "Who needs those selfish relatives," he said to himself. "I have real friends now."

Jeff drifted off to sleep and after what seemed like an eternity, he woke up. Jeff was not in his nice big mansion. He was not in his huge bedroom with the high ceiling. There was none of the familiar surroundings. He was in a hospital room. He rose, looked around and tried to remember something, or anything, that would make sense of the situation.

At that moment a doctor walked in with a nurse. "Well, I see you've finally come to," he said as he put a stethoscope to Jeff's chest. "You've been in a coma for the past week. Do you remember anything?"

It was beginning to come back to Jeff now. "Oh yeah," he said hesitantly, "I think I remember now. I was walking across the street when...." That's all he remembered.

"You were hit by a car crossing the street," the nurse said.

"You're very fortunate," the doctor said as he checked his pulse. "You had a bad concussion, but you seem to be fine otherwise. I think you can be released in a day or two."

"Oh, by the way," the nurse added. "There's someone outside that wants to talk to you. He's a lawyer. Something about a will. He says you have just inherited a fortune. Want to talk to him now?"

THE JUNKYARD CAFE

Nobody thought the health department would approve a restaurant in the middle of a junkyard but it passed all the health inspections. It was such a unique display of genius that it was an instant success. People came from hundreds of miles around to experience the ultimate in dining experience. People had to make reservations for weeks in advance. Folks would come around just to see this freak of nature, an oasis in the middle of a junkyard, as it were. It even made it to the front page of "Curious Cuisine" magazine.

It all started many months ago when David Morgan decided to get into the restaurant business. It had always appealed to him to have his own restaurant but he just didn't have the time, the money or experience, to pull it off. Then he happened to meet Alex Cramer, a friend from work at the saw mill and suddenly the ball started rolling in his direction.

Alex had been in the restaurant business in a different city but left due to lack of funds and a sagging economy. The two discussed the idea over a bologna sandwich at lunch many times and it was the same old story. Not enough money. First you had to have a building. Then all sorts of hidden costs such as rent, hiring cooks and servers. And then there were lots of inspections that had to be done. And more expenses. The list went on and on and the idea was finally shelved indefinitely. Back to sawing lumber.

Then one day, Homer Mitchell decided to sell his junkyard business. The city had been on his back some time to dump the dump as nearby citizens were not happy at the unsightly view they had to endure. Not to mention the rats, snakes, briars, weeds, and other unsavory items that inhabited the property. And it smelled of grease and oil and rusting metal.

The neighborhood was beginning to prosper a couple of blocks from Mr. Mitchell but his immediate surroundings were stagnating. The junkyard had to go. It was inevitable and the slum clearance and urban renewal movement started moving in his direction in earnest.

Homer was tired of fighting city hall. He was about to give in to the pressure. The inevitable ordinance passed, And then there were the threats of fines for every day he failed to comply.

Mr. Mitchell could have taken it to court and probably won, saying it was unconstitutional, but he couldn't afford the attorney fees and Mayor

Slye and his supporters knew it. The pressure was on.

Homer was willing to sell the junkyard for a fraction of what the land was worth. A deal was drawn up between Mr. Mitchell and the city. If he could either sell it or clean it up, no more fines would be imposed. But how valuable would land be that was covered by rusted hulks, soaked in oil and grease, and reeking of the smells that you would expect at a service garage. The town wanted to buy it for practically nothing, fumigate, plow over and cover with sod, and disinfect. "It would make a nice little park for the children," said Mrs. Thompkins, one of the town officials.

Mr. Mitchell was not going to sell his junkyard to the city, no way would he do that. Not in a thousand years. There had been too many harsh words and hard feelings to allow that.

However, David and Alex approached Mr. Mitchell and decided to offer him some money and a deal. To their surprise, or maybe not, Homer was so willing to get the monkey off his back and, most importantly, to not let the city acquire it, he was willing to sit down and talk to Morgan and Cramer and take just about anything they offered.

But there was another problem. David and Alex only had about half of what Mr. Mitchell was asking. So, in a stroke of genius, David came up with a brilliant idea.

The three met on a rainy evening in the local cafe over a cup of coffee and a grilled cheese sandwich. They hatched out a plan. The three men, David, Alex, and Homer, would jointly own the property and put a restaurant on the premises.

When word got out, it was obviously much to the dismay of the mayor and others, especially the neighbors and the Beautification Committee. The panic stricken community regrouped and started to put more pressure on poor Mr. Mitchell.

The plan was so bizarre and inconceivable, it was dismissed as a bad joke and a type of harassment. The mayor called it a hair brained scheme and the city council consulted with their legal office to get an eviction notice and to start issuing fines immediately.

However, David, Alex, and Homer, had an ace up their sleeve. A young attorney named Francis Fogle got wind of this and decided to help out the trio of entrepreneurs. Mr. Fogle was young and inexperienced but felt empathy for the three rebels. He had been slighted by the Mayor on several issues, resulting in some hard feelings on both sides. The die was cast and the young upstart, trouble making attorney was on a mission.

"We won't let the city steam roll us," Fogle said as they met in his small apartment one evening. "You have rights and I'm here to see that those rights are upheld. I won't charge you anything for my work but I'd like to be a partner in the business. I have some funds that might help up get started. I think we have a collective axe to grind."

They all shook hands and decided to proceed. They started a campaign, starting with the adjoining neighbors and working their way outward from the junkyard. They assured the citizens that it was the lift the neighborhood needed to get it on its feet. A restaurant in the middle of Taft Street and 3rd Avenue. An eyesore would be magically transformed into a beautiful restaurant. "A park for children would be nice," Fogle stated. "But it won't bring money into the neighborhood. You can put a park anywhere."

It wasn't long until they had gotten support from the neighborhood. And they also got permits and started work on the "Junkyard Cafe." It was as if, as one reporter said, "a state of war exists." Just the type of stuff that sells papers. Taking on the establishment was something that appealed to most people, especially the blue collar groups. And the white collar crowd got on the bandwagon, too.

The mayor called it "Fogle's foibles." This was the fire the group needed. When this was printed in the newspaper, the community began to turn against Mayor Slye. Suddenly the establishment was the enemy of the people.

So, work started on the Junkyard Cafe and the "train wreck" was transformed into an outdoor-indoor restaurant selling "junk food." It was a sight to behold, as some of the wrecked cars were left as part of the decor, along with sheds and an old broken down bulldozer. They cleaned up the grease and oil and put up tables and chairs outside with candles and a view of what used to be. Landscaping transformed the grounds into a park-like atmosphere. The snakes and weeds were gone, replaced by shrubs and flowers. The broken down rusting fence was replaced by a stunning rock wall.

The Junkyard Cafe retained its charm. A view of what used to be intermingled with the new and improved. Even the Mayor had a change of heart. "Maybe I was wrong," he said in an interview. "I have reservations for this Saturday night."

As with most politicians, he straddled the fence of popularity, leaning whichever way the popular wind blew. A lesson in human nature was played out in many ways. Going with the flow and the tide was they way to win votes.

The Cafe was just as charming inside the new building, which was more like a museum with tables and chairs. Old relics from junkyards past lined the walls and overhead shelves. Transmissions, tires, hubcaps, steering wheels, dashboards, gearshifts, and other memorabilia, were for all to view while they dined on popular cuisine.

The menu was listed as "Junk Food," a term that Mayor Slye took credit for. It listed items such as Oil Pan Bean Soup, Transmission Stew, Chicken Clutch Casserole, and Scrapheap Salad. The utensils had handles that resembled screwdrivers and wrenches.

As time went on, the business grew. Other Junk Yard Cafes sprung up in nearby towns and cities. It became a thriving, multi-million dollar business.

And when election time came around, Homer Mitchell, once the derided scourge of the neighborhood and target for expulsion from the good town, ran against the incumbent, Mayor Slye. Mitchell won by a landslide. Justice was finally served...with a touch of class. And Mayor Mitchell never forgot his roots at the corner of Taft Street and 3rd Avenue.

The Dead Don't Always Die

Elmer Hickson was in the best of health and was a strapping mid 30's man that looked fit as a fiddle. But he had a hidden health problem. His heart experienced a glitch at the wrong time.

It was early afternoon in May when Elmer was in his basement workshop when he suddenly collapsed on the floor. His wife Edith found him approximately two hours later when she returned from shopping.

He was unconscious, eyes partially open, skin cold, and limbs stiff. She immediately called 911 and they pronounced him dead shortly after they arrived. Artificial resuscitation was of no use as Elmer was already showing signs of rigor mortis.

Shocked and stunned, his wife, or now widow, Mrs. Edith Hickson, went through the usual series of tortuous questions at the hospital. "No, he didn't show any signs of distress that day," she said to the coroner as she sobbed quietly. "He had a good breakfast this morning and was looking forward to spending time in his workshop while I went shopping. He was even whistling when I left for the store."

The coroner asked if he had any medical issues. "The doctor said he was in perfect health when he had his last physical only a month ago," she stated.

The coroner expressed his condolences as the body made its way to the morgue, covered in a white sheet. He wanted to have an autopsy done to see what exactly was the cause of death. There were no marks on the body and no reason to suspect foul play. It seemed a clear cut case of heart failure, possibly an aneurysm or maybe Atrial fibrillation.

Maybe even a massive stroke. The autopsy would tell the story, whatever it was.

The two lab assistants, Arnie Simpson and Bill Wickes, silently and leisurely wheeled Mr. Hickson's body down the lonely hallway, then into the service elevator to avoid disturbing hospital visitors. Down two floors and finally to the basement. Then, they pushed the gurney down the dimly lit tile floored hall and into the morgue. Parking it in front of the cooler, Mr. Hickson's body would have to wait it's turn for the autopsy. "There are two bodies ahead of this one," Simpson said solemnly, trying to be as respectful as possible.

"Yeah," Wickes responded. "Let's get a cup of coffee before we put this one in cold storage. It can wait."

The two lab techs left the morgue to go up to the cafeteria for a cup of coffee. It sounded really good after being in the cold morgue.

"They make good coffee here," Bill said as he sipped.

"You know," Arnie stated. "I never get used to taking bodies down to the morgue. Hospitals are supposed to cure people."

"Well," Bill responded as if he were lost for words. "We better get back to work."

They were gone about twenty minutes. When they returned, they were shocked.

Mr. Hickson was sitting up on the gurney with the sheet wrapped around him except for his head. He looked at the two boys and spoke. "What the heck am I doing here. And where is here?"

"Somebody is playing a joke on us," Arnie said with a laugh.

"Yeah," Bill said with a nervous forced smile. "I bet it's Tom from pathology."

"I don't know what you're talking about," Hickson said with a disturbed look on his face. "It's cold in here and I want to know what's going on. Can you turn the heat up?"

"Who are you, sir?" Arnie asked as he walked over to the man in the sheet.

"I'm Elmer Hickson." The two boys laughed.

"Who are you really?" Bill said.

"I'm Elmer Hickson. Who are you?"

The two assistants walked over and took a closer look. His toe tag was still attached and they looked at the man who said he was Elmer Hickson. He was beginning to get some color in his face.

Turning a bit pale, Bill Wikes stated soberly, "I know this is going to sound crazy but I think it really is Mr. Hickson."

"Of course it's me. What am I doing here?"

"I didn't get a good look at his face," Arnie stated, still not believing it's Hickson as he looked carefully at the so-called "corpse."

"How do you feel?" Tom asked.

"A bit weak, cold and stiff but otherwise okay," Hickson answered.

"We thought you were dead," Arnie said as he felt Hickson's skin.

"Better get Doctor Ramsey," Simpson said.

"I don't need a doctor," Hickson said impatiently.

Bill dashed out the door and summoned the doctor to take a good look at the would be corpse.

The doctor hastened into the chilly room as Hickson wrapped himself tighter in the sheet. Dr. Ramsey slowly looked at Mr. Hickson from a distance and affirmed it was indeed Elmer Hickson. The doctor approached him and nervously placed the stethoscope on his chest.

"He seems to be alive and well," Dr. Ramsey said. "No doubt about it. His heart sounds fine to me. Pulse is strong."

"I'm cold and hungry," Hickson said as he lowered himself from the gurney and touched his toes on the cold, tile floor. "What happened? Have I been in an accident or something?"

"Well," the doctor said. "I don't know where to begin."

"Got any coffee around here?" Hickson asked.

"I don't understand," Dr. Ramsey said as he was quietly shaking his head. "You're supposed to be....dead."

"Nonsense," Hickson said. "If I was dead, I wouldn't be talking to you."

"It can't be," the doctor stated to the two assistants. "I checked him out earlier and there was no sign of life for four hours."

"Well, we all make mistakes." Hickson said as he started walking stiffly toward the door. "Where's Edith? Is she ok?"

"Oh," Dr. Ramsey said with a tremble in his voice. "She's in my office filling out forms. I'll go get her."

As Mrs. Hickson arrived, she almost fell over. The two assistants had to keep her from falling onto the floor.

"My Gosh," she said with a start, clutching her chest. "He's alive."

She ran over to him and embraced him and felt of his arms. She looked into his eyes and saw there was definitely life there. "How do you feel?"

"A little tired and thirsty," he answered. "But otherwise, O.K. I guess."

"Do you remember anything during the last four hours?" Dr. Ramsey asked.

"Not a thing," Hickson answered. "I guess I was asleep."

"You can say that again." Arnie said under his breath.

Dr. Ramsey insisted that Mr. Hickson be thoroughly examined before being released.

"I guess that means he doesn't get an autopsy," Bill Wickes whispered to Arnie with a snicker.

Elmer was wheeled to a room where he spent a couple of days, having tests run. Several people, including nurses, doctors, lab techs, and CNAs, asked the same question Dr. Ramsey asked. What was it like being dead? What do you remember?

Elmer tried to answer with honesty. He repeatedly said, "I'm not sure. I'm starting to remember some things. You know, like a dream when you can remember parts of it and not other things."

"Can't you be more specific?" they would ask.

"Well," Elmer would say, "I'm really sort of tired right now. I'll try to be more specific later when my minds clears up more. Just give me more time to sort it out."

The inquirers would walk away disappointed.

Elmer Hickson was examined from head to toe, inside and out. Finally, Dr. Ramsey entered his hospital room where he and Mrs. Hickson were talking. Elmer was finishing up on his lunch. "How do you feel?" the doctor asked.

"I feel fine, Doc. Can I go home now."

"I don't see why not," the doctor exclaimed.

"What happened to me, anyway?" Elmer inquired.

"We're pretty sure that you had an atrial fibrillation episode. Your heart started beating uncontrollably and you.....well, to put it bluntly, you died. I'm giving you some medicine and it probably will never happen again."

Elmer and Edith were listening carefully. "That's ridiculous," she added. How could he die and come back to life?"

"There are some things in medical science we don't understand," the doctor added. "He was pronounced dead and was actually dead for about four hours. But the important thing is, he's back with us, alive and well."

"Can I finish my lunch," Elmer inquired. "The food here is pretty good."

"Sure, Mr. Hickson. I'll start the discharge procedure and you'll be home by the middle of the afternoon.

Elmer Hickson was discharged and Edith drove him home. He got his medicine and felt fine. In fact, he wanted to finish the project he started when he had his health problem. When supper was ready, he went back upstairs to the dining room and they had a good meal.

"I fixed your favorite," Edith said with a warm smile. "Steak, baked potato, and green beans."

"Yummy," Elmer answered. "I was getting hungry."

When dinner was over, they lounged in the living room and Edith asked, "Do you remember any more about when you were…gone?" she asked.

"Some of it is coming back to me," Elmer said, as he sipped on a cup of coffee.

"I remember seeing little orbs of light, then they kinda merged into one big bright light. And then I crossed over."

"What do you mean when you 'crossed over?'" she asked.

"It was like I was traveling through space or something and time didn't seem to have any meaning. Sort of like I was living in infinity."

"And then what happened?" she asked.

"That's all I can remember so far," he added. "But I'm gradually remembering more and more."

As word spread of this physiologically impossible phenomenon, the news media got a hold of the story. And they paid an inevitable visit to Mr. Hickson a few days later.

He and Edith welcomed them into their home and saw the famous basement where it all started. Edith filled in the reporters on the sequence of events. It was all very interesting but the real reason the reporters were there was to find out what Elmer experienced during those mysterious four days.

"I'm gradually beginning to remember a few things," Elmer said to the lady from the newspaper.

"What can you tell us?" she asked as she put her pen to the pad.

"Well, those four hours were sort of like a lifetime. I mean it was like time didn't exist. Do you understand?"

"Tell me more, Mr. Hickson."

"That's all I can say right now."

"We'll be back," the reported stated.

Later that evening as he and Edith were sitting in the living room, he said something that startled Edith.

"I haven't told you this," Elmer said. "But there were things that happened when I died that I can't tell you or anybody else. It was wonderful and I wish I could tell you but some things just have to remain a secret. If people knew how wonderful death was, there would be no reason for living in this world. I did not want to come back to this life but I came back for a reason and it wasn't to finish my project in the basement."

The Evil Old Man

Jaspar Wiggins lived in the big house on the hill, just on the outskirts of town. He lived alone and was not the type to associate with other people in the town of Glenville. He spent most of his time alone in the big house. How he spend his time was a mystery. Some say he had a laboratory in his basement where he performed scientific experiments. Other say he spent his days keeping watch on his property with a large telescope that peered out of his living room window.

He was also known by other names given to him by children in the neighborhood, such as "Old Grouch, Old Man Wiggins, and the Evil Old Man on the Hill, and Wiggy." These unflattering nick names were probably the result of Wiggins chasing the kids off his property for no good reason. They never disturbed or hurt anything on his property but Jaspar didn't like sharing it with anybody.

His estate stood high above a vacant lot known as Thompkins Field. which Mr. Wiggins owned. This was an ideal spot for a little league baseball field that the town needed badly, however Jaspar was not about to sell it or donate it for such a philanthropic reason.

Jaspar Wiggins was tall and thin. He seemed to always wear dark clothes that went with his thinning dark hair that was beginning to turn gray around the temples. He also had a pointed nose that some say looked somewhat like the end of a letter opener. He had high cheek bones and all that made him resemble Ichabod Crane. His intense gray eyes were piercing and he appeared to be looking right through a person. This led to another nickname called "undertaker." No one ever saw him smile but the scowls were plentiful.

He would make weekly visits to the grocery store and never engaged in idle conversation. He would simply buy his goods, hand the money to the cashier, and leave. His expression never seemed to change.

His apple trees were a constant bother to him as he was always running off children who ventured into the orchard to steal a few apples. This became a game with some of the children. Eventually, Mr. Wiggins put up a barbed wire fence to keep out the pesky kids who thought it fun to pester poor Jaspar who would come storming out and throw a few free apples at the children as they ran away. "Get off my property!" he would yell. "I'll have the law on you." Then he'd shake his fist at them as they laughed and ran away.

Getting back to Thompkins Field, the town of Glenville tried many times to put in that well needed little league baseball field but Wiggins flatly refused. He had no need for all the noise and laughter that was associated with baseball and children. Besides, what did they ever do for him.

Jaspar was a wealthy man of whom most people in Glenville knew very little. He moved there ten years ago from Starksburg, some 200 miles to the north, and the information that was acquired about him was just enough to raise some eyebrows. Glenville's residents, like in most small towns, knew everybody's business, and Wiggins was no exception. It was found out that he made a fortune in the banking business along with other lucrative endeavors. Investments along with stocks and bonds put him in the upper economic echelon. It was also believed that he was not above foreclosing on a mortgage at a whim, leaving a family out in the cold. The almighty dollar had a special attraction for Mr. Wiggins, it was believed. And now that his fortune was made, he simply preferred to be left alone on his pile of wealth, which must have kept him warm at night.

Of course much of this view of him from the townspeople could have been somewhat embellished. Mr. Wiggins played the part of the wealthy eccentric. Living in his fortress on the hill even enhanced the view from below.

Halloween was especially stressful for Jaspar. trick or treaters never ventured up to his door for they feared him. He surely must have had traps set up around his house for the little masked goblins. Maybe a net to fall on unsuspecting treaters like a huge spider web. Then he would probably drag them off to his dungeon for scientific experiments, never to be seen alive again, except maybe as a zombie.

And the religious community had given up on him, too. When he first moved into the big house on the hill, he was visited by members of the churches, only to be turned away with a slamming door to the face. He had no need for religion or the churches that served the community, as he thought they were only after his money for their self serving endeavors.

When Thanksgiving rolled around, he had quit watching the Macy's Christmas parade on TV like he used to enjoy. Instead, he would buy a turkey TV dinner with cranberry sauce. This was his big Thanksgiving dinner. He would imagine people in the town having a large spread for the families. It was especially a lonely time for him as he thought about his own grandmother's house in the country. He would find himself singing softly, "over the river and through the woods, to grandmother's house we go." With a nip in the air and maybe a few snow flurries, he would almost be there again in his mind. Then, mercifully, the day would be over and it was business as usual. Looking out the window at the stark reality of the barren trees, the biting wind, and the sharp nip in the air, brought him back to his own lonely situation.

Christmas season was a time for Jaspar to remain at home as much as possible. The ringing bells of the Salvation Army beckoned him to throw a few coins in the pot. He would scurry past them, avoiding eye contact. "Merry Christmas," they would say cheerfully to him. He would pretend he didn't hear them at all. 'They're saying that just aggravate me,' he thought.

And the stores were alive with people hurriedly shopping and they got in his way. Those gifts they were buying were a waste of good money. Buying things that people didn't need just for the sake of buying gifts. 'It's ludicrous,' he would think. He was glad he didn't have to worry about buying gifts for he had no one to buy gifts for. The Christmas music was especially annoying to Jaspar. His mind would occasionally drift back to earlier childhood days when those songs really meant something. But now, they were just an annoyance that he would rather not hear.

He was really glad when Christmas was over. Another stressful time was behind him. Now he could actually celebrate New Years eve in his own way but it never seemed to be a time to celebrate. Older but not wiser. Maybe a little lonelier. His hair was a little grayer. Possibly a time for reflection but not much to reflect on except his big pile of money. He looked at his portfolio and it just stared back at him. It never spoke except in dollars and cents.

But his little single serving bottle of champagne with cheese and crackers would always make its way to the living room coffee table for him to consume. Then, off to bed before the clock struck midnight. He always heard the fireworks explode as he lay in bed trying to drift off to sleep. They seemed a long way off but he could see the flashes through his curtains.

And so it went, year after year. A routine that seemed to never end. Then one day in March, his hallowed ground was invaded by two little boys and a girl that thought it would be fun to make their way over the barbed wire fence and run the gauntlet. The plan was to sneak over the fence, run through his orchard, scale the brick wall, dash over the shrubs, and on to freedom on the other side of the hill where they would be home free. The highway was the DMZ, the goal for this commando mission. Surely old Wiggy would come storming out with his stick and chase them down the other side. But once they reached highway 42, their mission would be over. What a great story that would be to tell at school. No one had ever dared go that far or challenge the super power on the hill.

And the big day finally arrived. They worked up courage and the three commandos sneaked over the barbed wire fence and started their journey. The girl tripped over a root but they two boys helped her up and on they went. What courage that must have taken to cross the battlefield.

Just as they started to cross the shrubs, a giant figure appeared with glowing, piercing eyes. It was Jaspar. With fist in the air, he suddenly let out a bellow that could be heard ten miles away it seemed.

"Get away, you kids. You're trespassing on my property. I'll have you all put away in a reform school for this."

Just then he lunged forward as the kids turned around and went head over heels the way they came. The little girl was screaming and the boys went faster than they had ever run before. They could almost feel the hot breath of Mr. Wiggins as he closed in on the little trespassers.

Just as they reached the barbed wire fence, they started over but something terrible happened. Little Joe Martin was caught. The other two somehow managed to escape. Jaspar reached him and realized that young Martin was seriously injured.

Blood was gushing from his arm as he lay struggling and terrified over the barbed wire fence. The look of terror in his eyes was one of nightmarish horror. Surely, he thought, Mr. Wiggins would beat him to death or drag him off like a lion retrieving his helpless prey.

When Jaspar saw what had happened, he reached down to survey the damage and saw the emergency that was unfolding before him. Joe Martin had severed an artery and was bleeding profusely.

"Don't kill me, Mr. Wiggins," Martin said in a panicked, trembling voice.

"I'm not going to hurt you," Wiggins said compassionately as he he reached in his pocket.

Wiggins then took out his handkerchief and used it as a tourniquet on Martin's arm, stopping the bleeding. All thoughts of terrorizing the young kids vanished now. He was doing what he had to do to save the little boy's life.

Now in shock, Joe was no longer struggling but was simply helpless in the arms of Jaspar Wiggins, the tyrant of the hillside fortress.

Meanwhile, the other two children ran for help. Somehow, they thought, this commando mission went terribly wrong. The police was summoned along with the rescue squad.

Mr. Wiggins had gently picked up Joe and had taken him up to his house. He placed him in a lawn chair in his yard and was in the process of calling the rescue squad when he heard sirens coming up his driveway.

They whisked Joe Martin to the hospital and his prognosis was excellent. A transfusion of blood, a few stitches, and he would be good as new.

Soon, word got around that Jaspar Wiggins had saved the life of one of the neighborhood children. As Joe Martin lay in his hospital bed recovering, he related the story to his parents and fellow students who hovered by his bedside. "I guess it was a stupid thing for us to do," Joe said to his mother. "We should have stayed away from Mr. Wiggins' house."

Then suddenly, the biggest surprise of all. Jaspar appeared in the hospital room.

Stunned, they stared at Wiggins as Jaspar spoke to the young lad.

"How are you doing?" Joe answered with a gentle smile. A smile the town had never seen before.

"Doing great, thanks to you," Martin said with a smile.

"I'm afraid I've not been a very good neighbor," Wiggins stated. "I've turned into a hermit. A recluse. You see, I've developed a great distrust of people over the years."

Martin responded, "We shouldn't have been trespassing on your property, Mr. Wiggins. I'm sorry about that."

The room was silent for a few moments as the startled people just wondered what had come over the old grouch. Jaspar sat on the edge of the bed and spoke to Joe. "I understand you need a baseball field."

"We sure do, Mr. Wiggins," Joe answered as he perked up.

"Well, you shall have it. In fact, I'm donating Thompkins Field for that very purpose. It should be ready just in time for baseball season to start."

Jaspar Wiggins became the best friend that Glenville ever had. He came out of his reclusive life to help the homeless, assist the needy, and even played Santa Claus at Christmas. He started going to church and donated money to buy a new steeple.

He tore down the barbed wire fence and made the apple orchard open to the public. His generous deeds were many for he had a dramatic change of heart. The no-trespassing signs were removed.

Wiggins invited the whole town to his house for a big Christmas party. The largest party the town had ever seen. It became a yearly event. His Christmas lights were spectacular and drew crowds from miles around.

Halloween was a special event, too His elaborate decorations made headlines in the local newspaper and on the television station. He made a "house of horrors" in his basement for the whole neighborhood to enjoy.

Trick or treaters were treated to the best treats they had ever had.

The lessons learned were many but perhaps the most important was that even out of a disaster, miracles can happen. It was all a bit strange but so was Mr. Wiggins in his own way, that is until they really got to know him.

The baseball field was built that spring just like he promised and was unanimously re-named "Wiggins Field." Jaspar paid for all of it. On opening day, Joe Martin hit a homerun that landing right in the middle of Jaspar's orchard that, at one time, was off limits to the world.

It also appeared that Old Man Wiggins hit a homerun for both himself and the town of Glenville.

THE ISLAND

The guest list included Corey Jones, ex-marine and survivalist, Janet McAllister, waitress, Karen Wilkes, bank manager, and the captain of the pleasure cruiser "Margie Q," Tom Willett. The place was Calamari port in Hawaii. Although they didn't know each other, their only common bond was that they were all headed north to a small island where they were to meet their respective families, all of whom were staying at the same hotel.

The boat ride was going to be about two hours long. The chartered boat was less expensive than flying and seemed like a lot more fun. They quickly got to know one another as they plied through the beautiful blue Pacific waters.

Corey was a tall, muscular man with a vast knowledge of survivalist techniques. He was very curious about the various marine life around the islands. He was also interested in running a marathon later in the year. He was friendly and knowledgeable.

Janet was a blond haired, blue eyed girl, trying to earn enough money to move from a small town in Arizona to Las Vegas where she hoped to get a good job in a casino. Later, she hoped, she would go to college and study economics.

Karen was more reserved with a serious demeanor. A lot more mature and a few years older than Janet with medium length brown hair and dark brown eyes. Her good job as office bank manager earned her a good living. She was somewhat standoffish at first but warmed up to Corey and Janet, and before long they were conversing about all sorts of things. She had brought a briefcase with her, presumably to put in some work in her spare time.

Tom Willett kept to himself, keeping his eye on the ocean and his hands on the wheel. He was short and a bit overweight with a three day old beard. He wore a tee shirt and blue jeans and his hair was thinning on top. He knew these waters and reefs like the back of his hand. He glanced occasionally to the west and seemed a bit concerned about the gathering clouds in the distance.

"I'm not sure I like the way those clouds look," Corey stated with some seriousness. "They're gathering up a storm."

"It won't effect us, will it?" Janet asked as she looked at Corey with confidence.

"I don't know yet," he answered as he watched the direction of the clouds.

Karen kept quiet but grasped her briefcase as if she was worried it might get lost.

As they continued their journey, the waves increased somewhat and the boat was being tossed around. Tom kept the Margie Q on course as it cut through the water. The wind picked up and it became evident that the storm was getting closer.

"Maybe we should head for shore," Janet said nervously as she looked to the west.

"No need for that," Tom answered. "I've seen a lot worse than this."

Corey noticed some white caps on the waves as their small boat heaved and pitched, not being as much fun on the water as it was earlier as the rain began to fall and the wind picked up noticeably.

"Maybe you folks should go below for a while," Tom announced. "It won't be too much longer till we're in port."

"I think you girls should put on your life jackets," Corey said as he reached for his. "Just to be on the safe side." Corey the noticed a small life raft in the rear of the boat.

As the passengers began to go below in the cramped area under the bridge, the waves got higher and the winds increased.

"These storms sure come up suddenly," Karen said as she grasped her briefcase even harder. "It's making me a bit nervous."

Then there was a loud sound on the port side as the boat heaved over to the right throwing each of the passengers on top of one another.

Janet screamed. She scrambled topside as the others followed. A wave crashed over the bridge, drenching everyone with a healthy dose of salt water. Joe was nowhere to be seen.

"My God, where's Joe?" Janet inquired as they all started looking around.

Corey grabbed the wheel as the tiny boat was now out of position and was parallel to the crashing waves. Before Corey could turn the boat around into the waves, another wave pushed the boat over, capsizing it.

They all splashed into the water as the Margie Q lay upside down and began to sink. The waves were getting higher. Somehow, Corey managed to get into the life raft and work his way toward the girls. It required a super human effort but he got to Karen first and pulled her into the raft. Janet and Joe were nowhere to be seen. They searched and called out their names but no answer.

For the next fifteen minutes, which seemed like hours, they scanned the water around them as the raft bobbed up and down among the waves. There was no trace of Joe or Janet. Then, finally they spotted a life jacket. Rowing toward it through the choppy water, they reached Janet and pulled her aboard. She was semi conscious, exhausted, and apparently had ingested some salt water. Otherwise, she seemed in pretty good shape considering what she'd been through. She began to speak

"What happened," she asked groggily.

"You're safe now," Corey said as he cradled her in his arms.

Corey and Karen explained the situation as they were drifting out to sea with no sign of land, boats, or airplanes.

"Where are we?" Janet asked.

"I don't know," Corey answered. "But I'm sure they will be looking for us out here. The storm seems to be subsiding."

"I sure hope so," Karen added. "At least we're safe now."

Janet showed some signs of distress from drinking salt water but Corey gave her some fresh water. "It's a good thing we have some emergency rations on this raft," Corey added.

"But where is Joe?" Karen asked worriedly. She looked all around and could not see anyone.

"I don't know," Corey said. "But we'll keep looking. We seem to be pretty far out to sea now. And we have some flares, too. At the first sign of a boat or plane and we'll fire one off."

The three drifted for several days. The rations were a big help but were running out. Corey helped the two girls and gave them most of his share of the food and water. He was beginning to show some signs of dehydration.

"I'm calculating the we're drifting north west," Corey said. "I think there's a small island in the direction we're drifting." Corey seemed to be able to read the stars and through some mental calculations, headed the raft to the south east with the two paddles and the help of Janet and Karen.

This gave some hope to the girls but Corey was really not sure where they were. 'I don't understand why we've not seen a search plane or boat by now,' he thought to himself.

They continued to drift but early on the seventh morning, Corey woke up the girls to make an announcement.

"Land ho !!!" he shouted. He stood up in the raft as the girls woke up and began to scan the horizon.

"I see it," Janet said. "it must be Hawaii."

"I see it too," Karen added.

"I don't think it's Hawaii," Corey added. "But it is land and that's better than drifting out here in the middle of the Pacific Ocean."

Corey got the two paddles and he and Karen began to propel the raft in that direction. When Karen got tired, Janet took over. They were getting closer and they could see trees and birds.

"That's a good sign," Corey said. "Trees usually mean food and there's probably some fresh water, too."

Finally, they got to the sandy shore and made landfall. They pulled the raft up on the beach, climbed out and collapsed on the warm, dry sand.

"I think we're going to make it," Janet said confidently but weakly. She smiled for the first time in days.

"I think you're right," Corey added. "But we have a lot of work to do. We have to build a shelter and look for water and food."

"I'm too tired to do any of those things," Karen said as she stayed glued to the sand.

Corey left the girls on the shore and as they slept, he scouted the island. He was able to find what he thought was a source of fresh water. There were coconut trees and some wildlife. He pulled the raft farther in and began looking for something to build a shelter. He was dehydrated, after giving most of his water to the girls. He thought maybe water would be the first thing he would look for.

Fortunately, there was a shovel in the raft and he began digging under some trees that looked damp. After about half an hour, he reached some wet soil. Then some running water. He scooped up the precious liquid and after some time, he quenched his thirst.

By now, Karen and Janet had awoken. They looked for Corey but he was nowhere to be seen. Panic set in as Janet screamed and started running into a thicket, tripping and falling. She cut herself on something sharp.

Corey emerged from a stand of trees and saw Janet lying in the sand, bleeding.

"What happened to you?" he asked. "You're bleeding."

Corey then stopped the bleeding and calmly bandaged her with supplies from the raft.

"You saved my life again," Janet stated.

"I don't know what we would have done without you," Karen added.

"I do have some experience in survival techniques," Corey said as he put up his first aid supplies.

"I found water," he said. "I think we'll be fine until a rescue party finds us."

"We sure are lucky to be alive," Karen added. "And we owe it all to you. How did you find this island?"

"I recall seeing some small islands on a map some time ago. We just happened to be drifting toward them. The currents and the paddles did the rest."

Corey, with the help of Karen and Janet, built a shelter for all three to sleep in. He cut bamboo just the right lengths and was able to bend them into supports by cutting part of the bamboo. He made a cover for the hut with palm fronds and tall grass.

He dug up small worms and bugs to use as bait and was able to catch fish. He built a fire using friction. The fish cooked up perfectly and they enjoyed it. He put damp palm fronds on the fire to create smoke so it could be seen miles away in case a boat or plane was nearby. He built spears and a bow and arrow for hunting, in case they saw some wild game that would be suitable food.

He even used his shovel to spell out the letters "SOS" in the sand at the beach. He had two flares that he was saving in case they spotted a plane or ship.

Then one day, Karen was getting some water and a large lizard lunged at her. She dived backwards and, fortunately, Corey saw this in time and killed the reptile with his knife before it could bite her. They cooked the lizard over an open fire that evening and decided it tasted pretty good.

As the days wore on, the two girls started getting somewhat despondent. "I don't think we're ever going to be rescued," Janet said with her head hung down.

"Now let's don't lose faith," Corey would say. "It's just a matter of time before we're found."

Then Corey began being a bit secretive. He told the girls he was working on something on the far side of the island and for them to stay on the other side, near the hut till he was finished. He would be gone for over an hour at a time, then return with his shovel and axe.

"What are you doing over there?" Karen asked one day.

"It's a surprise for you two," he would answer. That's all they could get out of him.

"I wonder what he's up to?" Janet asked Karen one day while Corey was gone.

"I don't know," Karen answered. "Maybe he's building us a beach front cottage." They both laughed.

As the days followed, Corey spent more time alone on the other side of the island but came back in plenty of time to do any chores necessary for their comfort and survival. He kept the signal fire going and would put wet palm fronds on it from time to time and told the girls to stay there while he was gone so they could fire off the flare gun if case they saw a ship or plane.

The girls decided they would, in fact, investigate Corey's project on the other side of the island. They would sneak over there while Corey was fishing and take a look. They managed to get away for a few minutes and what they saw made their blood run cold. There was a large hole in the ground that looked like a grave. It was about six feet long by three feet wide and six feet deep.

Karen gulped," He's building a grave for us. He's planning to kill us and bury us here."

Janet was speechless as her knees felt weak.

"What are we going to do?" she asked in a quivering voice.

"Only one thing for us to do," Karen answered. "We have to kill him first before he kills us."

"But how do you know he's planning to do that?" Janet inquired.

"What else could it be?" Karen added. "Why would he be so secretive?"

"But how are we going to do that?" Janet inquired.

"We will have to use one of those spears he made for us. Catch him when he's not looking."

The next morning, Corey asked Janet to walk over to see what he's been working on.

"Oh, I don't think I want to see it, whatever it is." she answered.

"Don't be silly," Corey stated. "It's nothing that will hurt you. Let's go. Karen, you stay here and watch for ships or planes. We'll be back in a few minutes and you can see it, too."

Corey gently took Janet's arm as she looked back at Karen with terror in her eyes. When they were out of sight, Karen grabbed a sharp spear that Corey was using for protection. She stealthily worked her way toward the area of the hole and saw Corey and Janet standing beside it.

Suddenly Janet made a run for it. As she ran, Corey stood there in amazement. "What's with her?" he said to himself.

Then, Karen lunged at Corey and stabbed him in the back with the sharp spear. Corey was killed instantly as the spear head penetrated his heart. He fell in the hole, hitting his head on a rock on the way down.

As Karen and Janet regrouped at their campsite, Janet was in tears.

"What did he say to you?" Karen asked.

"He didn't say much but something about catching a wild boar and having a big barbecue."

"Then why did you run away?"

"He reached for a knife and I was afraid he was going to kill me," she answered. "Then I saw that wild boar out of the corner of my eye."

Karen was speechless. Maybe they made a mistake. Could they

have let their imaginations run away with them. After all, he'd taken pretty good care of them.

The next day they buried Corey and smoothed over the grave the best they could. Janet was almost in a catatonic state. She would not speak or eat for two days and would only drink sips of water.

"You have to eat something," Karen said. "I'm responsible for all this. Don't blame yourself. Listen, we have to get our story straight. Let's tell the rescue party that Corey drowned while fishing in the surf. Maybe attacked by a shark."

Janet nodded but was not sure of anything except they had killed somebody, maybe needlessly.

In a couple more days, they saw a boat in the distance and fired off a flare. The boat made its way to the shore and landed. It was a pleasure craft. After seeing the two girls stranded on the island, they contacted the Coast Guard by radio, who arrived in a few hours.

Captain Alomar of the Coast Guard patrol boat led a party on the island and examined the two girls for injuries or any possible illness.

"They seem to be in pretty good shape," he announced to the rest of his crew. "Considering they have been on this island for a long time, they have fared very well."

After giving Karen and Janet food and water and tending to a minor infection that Janet had gotten, they conducted an inquiry. The captain of the coast guard boat knew about the four people that had been lost at sea. Joe's body was never recovered and they asked about Corey Jones after seeing some of his belongings on the beach. Karen and Janet had failed to hide those articles.

"I see Corey Jones was here," the coast guard captain said. "Where is he?"

"Well," Karen stammered, "I don't know. He just disappeared. I think he must have drowned."

"How does a survival expert drown?" the captain asked suspiciously.

After searching the island, they discovered a wild boar who had started to dig up Corey's grave. "I think we'll do some digging here," the Coast Guard captain said as some of his crew began to grim task of uncovering Corey's body.

One of the crewman notice a stab wound in his back and blunt trauma on his head.

"I think we'll have to do an autopsy," the captain said. "In the meantime, we are holding both of you on suspicion of murder."

A Dry Day In Vance

It was another hot and dusty Nebraska day in the town of Vance. The year was 1874 and the people's spirits were fading as fast as the water supply. The dust swirled here and there as the sun beat down upon them to remind the town that they were in the middle of another drought. Every summer they had experienced dry spells but not as bad as this one.

The corn was on the verge of drying up into little weed-like stalks and blowing away along with the hopes and dreams of the farmers and ranchers. But most important at the moment was the fact that the drinking water supply was dangerously low.

The Pinyon River was just a trickle now and could no longer provide the livestock with water. The wells were at an all time low and everyone was down to their last reserve..

Travel was slow and even if someone traveled miles for water, they couldn't bring enough to save the town. Some folks were already making plans to move on. Only the buzzards and crows seemed happy as they circled in anticipation of another carcass lying in the hot summer heat.

Town Sheriff Tyler had wired Silver City for assistance but the same condition existed there too. People were beginning to feel trapped in a hot dusty prison with no escape.

In the Gold Nugget Saloon, the boys were sitting at the tables playing cards trying to keep their minds off the increasingly desperate situation. There was still some whiskey left but it was not the same as water when you need it. All the beer was gone now as the cowboys walked into the saloon with disappointment. The saloon was always a haven from the harsh conditions that existed outside but now, the desperation was creeping inside.

Most of the stores were barely open and nobody was in much of a mood to spend money. The general store was still open and you could still find dry goods and a few cans of beans.

In the school house, mayor Jim Dooley and alderman J.R. Daniel, along with Sheriff Tyler, sat down to discuss what could be done. The sheriff exclaimed, "I vote to move the whole town to a new location. Women and children first, up to Fort Pedro. I know it's a hundred miles but it's in the mountains and I know they've got water there."

"But what about the horses?" Dooley asked "What do you expect them to drink for a hundred miles?"

J.R. Daniel, the hotel manager, pointed out that they should send out some volunteers to travel at night and look for possible springs. Maybe bring back a few barrels of water for the horses. They all finally agreed that moving the citizens was the only solution to the problem and was infinitely better than doing nothing at all. It was better than waiting to die in the hot sun.

Sheriff Tyler sat in the saloon that evening as a tumbleweed bounced it's way down the deserted street, paused for a moment in front of the saloon's swinging doors, then moved on. This was the first lawman's job Tyler had held and it looked like it might be his last. He thought about it. Those years he spent in the army wanting to be a town sheriff and for it to end like this. Tyler, even though he had given up hope of keeping that poor excuse of a town alive, had not shown it. He tried to stay upbeat and positive for the sake of morale. Right now it was his duty to protect the citizens. And their only hope was to move to another location but time was running out. His parched brow and dusty hair blended in perfectly with the scowl on his face. 'We'll ought to start moving the town soon," he thought. 'Best to travel at night.' He formulated a plan to evacuate the citizens but it had to be done while there was still time.

However, all of a sudden Jim Dooley raced into the saloon with some interesting news. "Sheriff, come quick. There's some dude out here claiming to be able to make it rain." Tyler had seen this kind before in the army. They were obviously thieves and rogues. His first reaction was to run this fellow out of town. Send him back to a circus somewhere. The nerve of a man preying on the emotions of a desperate town. But he thought again. What would be so bad about a man bringing some hope to a hopeless situation. That might be just what Vance needed. Some hope. Besides, while the town was being entertained, he and the town leaders could be setting up plans for the inevitable evacuation.

Tyler was the last one out of the swinging doors of the Silver Dollar Saloon as he calmly walked outside, boot heels clopping the wooden floor slats and spurs jingling.

This so called "rainmaker" had stopped outside the saloon in his covered wagon to attract attention and he certainly had. Already about twenty of Vance's residents were gathered around the wagon staring at a tall bearded man with a top hat. He looked a little like Abraham Lincoln. He stood up in the front of his covered wagon with his hands pressing anxiously against his vest pockets with his chin held upward as if to beckon a listening audience.

Seated beside this tall, mysteriously looking bearded man was an Indian. He wore a colorful headband and poncho made of wool. He sat staring horizontally into space, not making a single motion. He wore a stoic look of sincerity and peacefulness.

Sheriff Tyler sauntered silently toward the wagon as the crowd increased. Men, women, and children alike were mingled in the largest get together on Main street since the hanging of one of the Dalton gang back in '71.

The old man was waiting till just the right moment to speak as the sheriff walked nearer, showing the expression of a skeptic. His five pointed silver star gleaming in the hot mid day sun.

On the side of the covered wagon read "Rainmakers, Inc. Julius J. Corbett, Owner, Philadelphia, Pa."

When Tyler finally elbowed his way to the front of the group of curious onlookers, the old man finally spoke. "Citizen of the fair city of Vance, permit me to introduce myself. I am Julius J. Corbett, owner of the Rainmakers, Inc. Main office, Philadelphia. To my right is a gentleman named 'Hook.' He is my loyal associate and stock holder."

Hook did not flinch or even blink at this somewhat strange introduction. He just sat there stoically, not moving at all, not blinking his eyes and with his arms still folded.

The townspeople, silenced by this strange pair of men, could not afford to be too skeptical at a time like this. They were desperate and apparently Corbett and Hook knew it. He spoke, addressing first one side of the audience then the other.

"As I have traveled through this dust bowl you call a town, I noticed the parched fields and emaciated livestock outside of town. And I noticed a grave need for my services. Hook and I are specialists in rainmaking. We guarantee rain within three days. The audience mumbled and fidgeted nervously at this statement.

"All you have to do is pay us a nominal fee and we will get to work immediately. The standard fee is $500, paid in advance, of course.

Talk it over amongst yourselves and let us know in one hour." Corbett pulled out his pocket watch and noted the time.

Corbett and Hook then started to retire inside the wagon when Tyler spoke. "Wait a minute, friend. What you propose is pretty incredible. You make it rain first and then we'll pay you, although I don't think we can afford $500."

Corbett looked down at Tyler with a penetrating, cold stare with steely eyes. "Sir, you question our ability to make it rain?"

"Well, uh, it does seem a little far fetched." The crowd began to shake their heads in agreement. "I mean you come into town and make a speech about bringing rain in three days. Why are we supposed to believe this?"

"Sir, skepticism is no stranger to us. Every town we've been to has shown this attitude at first. We've never failed to deliver the goods, It's the same all over. Modern science had a slow beginning but you people have nothing to gain and everything to lose if you don't accept my offer."

One of the townspeople spoke, "Where have you brought rain before? I think we'll check this out."

"I'm not at liberty to give out that information," replied Corbett. "That's classified information."

Corbett paused and then stated, "We shall see you in one hour."

The mayor wormed his way to the front of the crowd. "We shall have a town meeting in the school house to decide what we're going to do. But first, I'm going to send a few telegrams to see if any other towns have heard of you. We're not buying a pig in a poke."

Corbett and Hook then retired to the confines of their covered wagon and drew the privacy curtain.

"We'll see you in an hour," the sheriff shouted outside the wagon as they started walking toward the schoolhouse.

Meanwhile, the telegraph turned up no information on the rainmaker. They checked with all the larger towns as well as smaller one. They had never heard of Corbett and his outlandish claims.

In the schoolhouse, tension was mounting. "What do you think of this fellow?" the mayor asked of Tyler.

"I think he's a fake," replied the sheriff. "I've seen fellows like this before. They see a desperate situation and take advantage of it."

"I'm inclined to agree with you," Mayor Dooley said. "He's probably got a hundred gallons of water in that wagon. I think we ought to storm it and see what's in there."

"Let's not lose our heads," Tyler said. "I want to see what the rest of the town thinks. At least this has gotten their minds off the drought for a while. Might be good for morale."

"Run him out of town!" rancher Bert Crandall yelled as he beat his fist against the table.

Luke Martin, owner of the saloon and hotel stated, "I've seen fakers like this before. They're leeches, parasites, scum. His promise doesn't mean any more than a handful of dust."

Like most of the citizens, they were skeptical but also desperate.

"I say we make him an offer," Marjorie Wickes stated. who was a highly respected member of the community and also the school teacher.

"Ok then," the mayor proposed, "let's take a vote."

After the voting by the citizens, it was decided that an offer would be the most logical solution but under certain conditions. "We obviously can't give them $500 but we can offer less." the mayor explained.

After it was decided to collect money, pledges were made and the total was only $175. Some gave on the spot while others had to either get money out of the bank or go home and get theirs.

The sheriff stated, "Just to be on the safe side, we'll place guards around their wagon 24 hours a day and if they try to abscond with our money, we'll simply get it back. They can't escape with it."

"Good idea," the town leaders agreed. Time was running out. With only five minutes to spare, they hurried back to the wagon to make their meager offer.

In the distance, a dust devil skirted ominously across the parched earth, spewing dust high into the air. It disappeared almost as quickly as it appeared.

Corbett and Hook had emerged and were sitting in their seat

in front of the wagon behind their horses as the group approached. Corbett dusted off his black hat and rose from his seat. "Well, gentlemen, what will it be? We don't have all day. We have other towns to save."

"Mr. Corbett," the mayor said as he coughed up some dust. "We couldn't afford $500. These are hard times."

"Very well," Corbett said, "we shall be going now."

"Wait," Tyler added, "we got $175. That's all we can afford."

Corbett stood perfectly still as his cold stare could have frozen a glass of whiskey.

"Maybe you could take this amount," Miss Wickes pleaded. "And we could owe you the rest. Besides, the whole town contributed all they could."

"Very well," Corbett finally acknowledged. "You are in grave need of moisture. The town of Vance will cease to exist without help. It may, however, take a little longer, you understand. But you shall have your rain within four days."

The crowd cheered, although they weren't quite sure why. They had only seen empty promises up to this point along with their vanishing money.

Mayor Dooley then spoke to Corbett and Hook, "We have a nice restaurant, saloon, and hotel down the street if you'd....." He was cut short.

Corbett then answered rather sharply, "Sir, we're here for a purpose. And that purpose if to make rain. We've brought our own food and water and we're not interested in mingling with people and availing ourselves of your services. We shall start scanning the area and begin our work at sundown." He accepted the bag of money and he and Hook disappeared again inside their wagon.

"I want 24 hour surveillance on this wagon," Sheriff Tyler said. He had no shortage of volunteers. Soon, the wagon was surrounded by armed men.

The sun was beginning to go down behind a ridge of mountains as the shadows stretched longer across the dusty street. A breeze picked up and the tumbleweeds were starting to move faster.

Suddenly, the two strange visitors emerged and started moving their wagon down the street as the crowd followed anxiously. When they got to the edge of town, they were looking over an expanse of desert that was barren and lonely looking. A few cacti could be seen in the distance and coyotes could be heard far off.

Corbett and Hook took out some strange looking instruments and were looking up in the sky. They were writing down things, who knows what. They would not discuss it with anyone. They took readings and measured distances between mountain peaks. They threw dust up in the air and wrote some more. They used a sextant as if they were trying to figure out where they were. Then, as it got darker that evening, they got back in their wagon and returned to their original place on Main Street. Without saying a word, they went inside their wagon as a faint glow could be seen shining through the canvas.

As the guards stood watch outside the rainmaker's wagon, it was quiet inside. Not a sound was heard all night. The only noise came from the Silver Dollar Saloon where the cowboys and gamblers were having the best time they'd had in weeks. It was almost like they were celebrating.

And as morning broke, Corbett and Hook came out of their wagon and began moving again. This time toward the other end of town. When they found a clearing, they brought out some more interesting things from inside the wagon, including a small cannon.

The sheriff was walking down the street when he noticed the wagon was gone. Tyler was not worried, though. He knew his guards were keeping close watch. J.R. Daniel came out of the hotel and gave Tyler some information. "Do you know what the rainmakers are doing this very minute? They have a cannon set up on the east end of town. I think they are going to blow something up."

Sheriff Tyler smiled, "I don't think there's anything out there worth blowing up but I'll check it out."

As Tyler arrived, half the town turned out. He confronted Corbett, "May I ask what you're doing?"

"Apparently," Corbett stated, "you and the rest of the town are not familiar with the science of rainmaking. First, we must send chemicals up into the stratosphere to make clouds."

Then Corbett pointed to some rockets that Hook had placed on the ground. Corbett continued, "These rockets are placed at just the right angle to serve the purpose of a catalyst. They will cause the clouds to form moisture and if the wind is right, you will have rain soon."

"And what if the wind is not right?"

Corbett pointed to a balloon that was filled with helium.

"Don't worry, sheriff, we'll calculated the speed of the upper atmosphere with this balloon. And also the humidity and barometric pressure. By my calculations so far, the conditions should be suitable in a couple of days."

"I sure hope so, for your sake," the sheriff answered.

Just then a rocket blasted off from it's launch in a cloud of white smoke. It startled the onlookers as they watched the projectile accelerate until it was out of sight. Then a faint explosion could be seen as it produced a faint blue cloud.

Then, a second rocket took off as it produced a pink cloud. Then another rocket with a green cloud. Corbett was busy taking notes. And more strange instruments were brought out by Hook.

This went on most of the afternoon as many of the towns people made a day of it, bringing picnic lunches to watch the fireworks display.

"We may not get rain but it's been fun to watch," Miss Wickes noted with a smile.

For the next two days, there were more rockets and cannon blasts. A reddish haze hung over the town of Vance for a few minutes. It even obscured the sun for a few seconds.

On the evening of the third night, the town was getting restless. It was time for action. They'd had enough fireworks and strange metallic instruments probing the sky. They had seen these two mysterious people wander around the edge of town, rarely speaking but keeping to their work. Now, they wanted some rain. The situation was getting even more desperate.

"If we don't get rain in the next two days," said the sheriff, "I'm going to start evacuating the town."

The mayor concurred and was not happy with the way things were going, or rather not going. The sky was still cloudless and the sun was hotter than ever. "At least it's evening and it will get cooler."

"I believe this has been the hottest day of the summer," Dooley added with an air of despair as he wiped his brow. "I think we need to have a serious talk with those flim flammers."

Sheriff Tyler approached the wagon and announced, "Corbett, Hook, It's me, Sheriff Tyler. I want to come in a talk to you."

To the amazement of Tyler, Corbett responded, "Come in, Sheriff."

Tyler pulled open the flap and looked inside. Hook and Corbett were playing a chess game. There were metallic instruments and notebooks everywhere. Glass tubes and flasks lined the walls. Chemicals of all sorts and colors. Rockets and black powder. In the rear of the wagon was their cannon. Barrels of water caught the eye of Tyler as he thought how the town could sure use those.

"Sit down, sheriff," Corbett said as he moved a chess piece.

"I guess you're wanting to know when the rains will come."

"Well, that had crossed my mind," the sheriff responded sarcastically.

Hook turned up the flame on the kerosene lamp so it would be brighter in the wagon, "I really don't know," Corbett answered. "Your move, Hook."

"Well now that's not the answer I was looking for," Tyler answered.

"Look, sheriff, we can only provide the atmosphere with the necessary materials for the proper reactions. It's up to nature now. It will rain, I'm sure, but it may take a little longer than expected. Besides, you only gave us $175. These chemicals cost money, you know. We have a lot of overhead expenses."

"Well, what can I tell those restless people that are waiting for the rain you promised?"

"Tell the town to just be patient a little while longer. Besides, if it doesn't rain, you get your money back so what's the problem."

As Tyler started to leave the wagon, he heard a commotion

outside. Then a panicky voice, "Sheriff, come quick. There's a fire on the other side of town."

Everyone rushed to the other end of town, including the guards who were assigned to watch Corbett and Hook. It was the livery stable that was burning. The fire brigade was quick to arrive with a tank of water. It was the last water reserve the town of Vance had. As they safely removed the horses, the buckets were brought out and in a while, the fire was brought under control. Unfortunately, however, they used the last amount of water reserve the town had.

"We saved the town but we lost the water," the mayor said as he brushed off the soot from his clothes.

"And still no sign of rain," the sheriff stated. He looked up at the sky for now night had fallen. The stars were shining brightly.

Harvey Kosta then came rushing up to the mayor and sheriff with some disturbing news. Out of breath, he spurted out, "The wagon's gone. They've left."

"You mean Corbett and Hook?" Tyler asked.

"Yes, the wagon is gone and there's no sign of them."

Arriving at the scene, they looked for tracks but saw none. They immediately rounded up a posse to chase down those criminals. "They'll be sorry they did this to us," Mayor Dooley said with vengeance in his voice. "I believe they set that fire as a diversion so they could leave under the cover of darkness."

The problem was it was now really dark. It was hard to track down anything now. The wagon could be miles from town, hidden in a cove. The would have to wait till day break.

An emergency meeting was called in the Silver Dollar Saloon to discuss what to do. By now, it was midnight, and much too dark to do anything. They assigned several posses to travel in different directions. They would spread out and cover every possible exit point then rendezvous back in town at noon.

The next morning, the angry townspeople gathered but saw no tracks to follow.

"I don't understand it," Sheriff Tyler said with bewilderment. "There's no tracks. "We'll just have to start out in different directions till be catch up with them. They can't be too far away. Covered wagons can't move very fast."

"We'll get our $175 back and then some," an angry Ben Phillips announced as he checked the bullets in his gun.

"They'll be sorry about this," Tyler said. "Corbett set a fire which is arson. Then, while we were all over there fighting the fire, they hightailed it with our money. Pretty clever."

"I never did trust them," Dooley added.

"I think the wind and sand has covered up their tracks," Tyler said as he looked around for any sign of the wagon tracks.

The five posses took off at first light and returned at noon. None of the groups of men found any trace of the wagon or even fresh tracks.

"It's like they vanished into thin air," Phillips said as he looked thirsty and tired.

Bud Martin, one of the leading ranchers then looked up and saw something. "There's a cloud on the horizon."

"So what," Tyler added. "Unless it has rain with it, it's of no use to us."

Then another cloud appeared, and another. Soon, the dark object was making its way toward the town of Vance. More clouds formed and the wind picked up and the air began to cool.

Marjorie Wickes, upon hearing a clap of thunder said. "I think a storm is headed this way."

This was the announcement the town was wanting to hear. They all looked up and saw dark clouds headed their way. More thunder and then bolts of lightning.

Could it be? Then, as if an angel from Heaven was touching their faces, they felt rain drops. Cool, refreshing life giving rain. Not much at first but it began to pick up. Soon, it was a drizzle. Then, like the miracle they were waiting for, the sky opened up. Folks were standing in the rain with their mouths open, taking in the pure precious fluid.

The horse's watering troughs were filling up. The river began to flow. The rain barrels were overflowing. For a few moments, no one thought of the rainmaker and his curious friend, Hook. Mayor

Dooley led a march down Main Street as the rains continued. Everyone was cheering. Cowboys were shooting their guns up in the air in celebration.

The town was saved. The people were saved. In the coming months, the crops began to flourish and the cattle ranches had plenty of grass for the livestock. Never again did Vance ever see a drought like that again. They always had plenty of water.

No one will ever know if the rainmaker was really the one who made it rain. Surely, it will always be a mystery and they never saw Julius J. Corbett and Hook again. They never had a need for them. One thing is for sure. It was the best $175 investment the town ever made.

THE SNOWS OF PINE MOUNTAIN

Cindy Wilson woke up from a deep sleep and found herself in unfamiliar territory. She might have been asleep for five minutes or five days, she didn't know. As she rubbed her eyes, she couldn't remember anything at first. Gradually, she began to realize that she was not in a familiar surrounding.

As she looked around the room she saw the interior of a rustic cabin and could smell a wood fire. As she glanced over to one side, she saw a fireplace with flickering flames. It looked nice and comforting. She could feel the warmth. There was an old chair leaned up against a wall and some pots and pans piled up on a table along with what looked like a diamond bracelet. There was a loaf of bread beside the pots and pans.

Leaning in the corner was a shotgun and hanging from the wall was an old overcoat. A couch was along one side of the wall with a ratty old afghan draped across the top.

As she scanned the room further she saw a window and noticed it was snowing outside. 'Where am I,' she thought to herself. 'What am I doing here and how did I get here?'

She tried to move but found it very difficult. Then she realized that she was injured. He left leg was apparently broken below the knee with a neatly covered with a bandage around it. Her right arm was very sore but she could move it freely.

Just at that moment, someone entered the cabin through the front door. She felt a blast of cold air as a man stood there holding an arm full of firewood.

He gently closed the door behind him, put down the wood, and suddenly realized that Cindy was awake. He looked over at her and smiled. "I see you have come to," he said in a calm soothing voice.

"I'm Morris Updike," he said as he introduced himself. "You've been unconscious for almost twenty four hours. How do you feel?"

"What am I doing here?" she inquired with some serious concern in her voice.

"You don't remember?" Morris said as he arranged the firewood in front of the crackling fireplace. He removed his red plaid cap and a blue overcoat and hung them on a peg along the wall next to the firewood. He was wearing blue jeans and a red sweatshirt. He had a beard and dark hair and was a good six foot four inches tall and very rugged looking. He had piercing blue eyes. Although he looked somewhat menacing, his voice was gentle and caring.

"I don't remember a thing, Mr. Updike," she answered.

Morris pulled up a chair next to Cindy. "You were in a plane crash, I'm sorry to say but you're safe now. Perfectly safe."

Cindy pondered for a moment and started to remember. "Now I remember," she stated as she thought. "We were flying along and then I heard a loud noise felt a tumbling sensation. I felt some pain and I guess I blacked out."

"The Cessna you were in crashed about two hundred yards away from here," Morris added as he held her hand gently. "Apparently, the pilot clipped the top of some trees. You were the only survivor. The other three people perished. I'm very sorry."

"My God," she said nervously. "Now I remember. I was lying there in the snow and that's the last thing I remember."

"I heard the crash," Updike explained as he rose from the chair. He went over to a table and poured Cindy a cup of coffee. "I went out to see what happened and you had apparently been thrown from the plane. I could see you had a broken leg and I fixed a splint and put you on a sled and brought you back to my cabin. I thought your arm was broken but I think it was just bruised badly."

"Where are we?" she asked.

"It's an area called Pine Mountain."

"Is a rescue party on their way up here?"

"Most definitely," Morris stated. "I don't have a phone myself but I found a cell phone in your pocketbook. I called 911 and they will be here tomorrow morning. I told them who you are and gave them the number on the tail section of the plane."

"How are they going to get through all this snow?" Cindy asked as she raised up as much as she could and looked at the white blanket outside.

"The snow is supposed to stop tonight. There is a good flat area about a hundred yards away. They're sending a helicopter tomorrow morning as soon as it's clear. It can land there and I gave them directions to my cabin. They can actually see my cabin from the clearing."

"That's good," Cindy said as she laid back down and sipped on her coffee. "Great coffee, thanks."

Updike looked at Cindy and asked, "Those other people in the plane, were they relatives of yours?"

"No," Cindy responded. "They were business associates except for the pilot. I didn't know any of them very well."

"Well," Morris added, "you'll be fine until tomorrow morning. They will fly you to a hospital about ten miles from here and take care of that leg. Your family will meet you there."

"I really appreciate you helping me," she stated. "Can I call my family?"

"Sure," Updike said as he handed her the cell phone. "But you better not talk long. Your batter is low and I don't have any electricity up here to charge it."

Cindy called her family and talked for a few minutes, assuring them she was alive and doing as well as could be expected even though she was in some pain. She then terminated the call in order to save the battery.

"I don't have any high powered pain killers," Morris said. "But I do have some headache powders and a bottle of whiskey."

"I'll take one of those powders," Cindy said as she welcomed the medicine. "I'll pass on the whiskey, though."

Morris gave here a headache powder and some good, clean cool water to wash it down.

"I have some soup if you're hungry," Morris said as he rose from his chair and went toward the wood stove.

"That would be nice," Cindy responded as she felt more relaxed. Morris seemed very easy going and friendly. His non-threatening nature made her feel very comfortable. They shared a bowl of vegetable soup and some bread.

"This soup is wonderful," she said.

"It's just some things I threw together. I'm not a very good cook but it doesn't take a master chef to make home made vegetable soup. It has carrots, chicken broth, celery, peas, and potatoes."

Late that afternoon the snow stopped. There was about two feet of snow on the ground.

"I think the snow has stopped a little earlier than expected," Updike said as he looked out the window. "Well, what do you know," he continued. "I just remembered. I have a nice bottle of wine that I had stored away for a special occasion. I can't think of a more special occasion than this. To celebrate the fact that you lived through a plane crash is pretty special, don't you think?"

"Wine sounds pretty good to me," Cindy answered. "I guess it is a special occasion that I survived but I really feel sorry for the others. She was feeling sympathy for their surviving families.

"I really feel bad for them," she said to Morris as she sipped on the wine.

"I know," Morris answered. "At first we're just glad to be alive but then you begin to think about the other people. Then it hits home."

"I hope you like the wine," Updike said as he poured himself a glass. "I'm not a wine connoisseur but it tastes pretty good to me."

"Tastes good to me, too," Cindy acknowledged. "Thank you for sharing it with me. I'll have to contact their families when I get to the hospital and tell them how sorry I was that all this happened."

Darkness fell on the little cabin on the hill as they continued to talk. Cindy told Morris about her job with a large law firm. At times she almost forgot about her situation. Morris was so easy to talk to.

Updike told Cindy about his life and the series of different jobs he had. He had worked on a fishing boat and was a carpenter. He's done work on an oil rig.

"My life has been pretty bland, you might say. Nothing spectacular. Just a lot of different jobs."

"How did you end up here?" she inquired.

"I'm just taking some time off," Morris said. "I have a job in Reidsville waiting for me in the spring. A friend of mine owns an auto repair shop and has promised me a job. Until then, I'll just hole up in this cabin and enjoy nature."

"That sounds pretty nice," she answered. "But don't you get lonely?"

"Yeah, I guess I do but sometimes people drop in for a visit."

They both had a good laugh. The wine was taking hold and she was getting sleepy.

"You better get some rest," Morris said as he stoked the fireplace. "You have a busy day tomorrow."

She slept very well and when she woke up, it was daylight. The sun was shining, and the cabin was bright and cheerful. The fire was warm and soothing. "Nothing to worry about now," she said to herself. She looked across the room and noticed that Morris was nowhere to be seen. She also noticed another blanket that he had placed on her sometime during the night. On a small table next to her was some water and another headache powder along with her cell phone and pocketbook. "I guess he's out getting more firewood," she said.

But Morris did not come back. It was eerily quiet in the little cabin except for the crackling of the fire. She began to get concerned. Minutes went by and then it must have been a half an hour and no sign of Mr. Updike. 'I wonder why he's taking so long to get back?' she thought to herself.

Then she thought that he was probably down at that clearing guiding in the helicopter. Suddenly she could head a sound in the distance and it sounded like a helicopter. It got louder and louder. She waited.

In a few minutes she heard footsteps on the small porch outside the cabin. A knock on the door was followed by several men dressed in white carrying a stretcher as they entered the cabin. It was the emergency personnel. They quickly introduced themselves and began taking her vital signs. First, her temperature was normal then her blood pressure seemed a bit high but not dangerous. They examined her leg and determined that she had a fractured tibia. She was not dehydrated. Her arm was just slightly bruised.

She asked about her new friend Morris Updike and at first there was no answer. Then, one of the EMS people explained to her that his name was not Updike but Big Sam Tyler, wanted for embezzling over a million dollars from a lucrative business he was working for. He'd already served ten years in the federal pen for counterfeiting. He had been holed up in the cabin and was waiting for an opportunity to make a run for it through the woods down to the railroad yard some five miles away."

"How did you know it was Tyler?" she asked.

"We knew because we had two eye witnesses from down the road that identified him and saw him heading this way with several large bags. They called us and we tracked him here. We were just waiting for the weather to clear so we could get here. We didn't want to tell you over the phone so you wouldn't worry. A fellow that would steal that kind of money might do anything to protect it. The sheriff and his deputies are outside right now looking for him. He shouldn't be hard to track with all this snow. I'm sure he's got a fortune in money with him. I hope we can recover it all."

"Well," said Cindy. "He was awfully good to me. Don't hurt him."

"He didn't hurt you, did he?" the EMS asked.

"No, he saved my life."

"Well I'm sure you ruined his escape plans. We're going to do a complete search of this cabin and we'll let you know when we find him."

Cindy was secured on a stretcher and transferred to the waiting helicopter and a short flight later she was in a hospital room awaiting surgery. He family was there and they heard about her ordeal. They were amazed to know that she was in the same cabin with a well known embezzler. And even more amazed that he took such good care of her.

"We even had wine and bread together," she stated. "I would have died out there if it hadn't been for Morris, I mean Big Sam."

In a short time the sheriff entered the room with some information.

"We followed Big Sam Tyler's tracks about two miles from his cabin. The tracks ended and we were unable to follow him any more. We have people around the train station and covering all the roads. We'll get him, you can be sure of that. We also recovered every bit of the money he stole."

"Where was the money?" she asked.

"It was sitting on a table in another room in plain sight. Almost like he wanted us to find it."

"How strange is that?" Cindy added.

Cindy looked a bit sad at her friend's plight and hoped he made it out of the snowy woods alive. She looked in her pocket book for a tissue and to her amazement she found the diamond necklace that she saw on the table in the cabin.

"Sheriff," she asked. "This necklace was in the cabin. I think you'd better take this as evidence. It's not mine. He must have put it there before he left."

"Why?" he inquired. "It's not part of the stolen articles. You can keep it if it wasn't stolen. We'll investigate it."

The sheriff examined it and stated that it must be worth a fortune. It had emeralds, diamonds, and rubies.

As winter turned to spring and spring turned into summer, there was still no sign of Big Sam Tyler. They combed the woods many times and never found a trace of him. It was almost like he had vanished into thin air where his tracks ended. Apparently, he had somehow managed to escape or maybe he died in a hidden part of the woods and would never be found. But Cindy hoped he was alive and would never be found for the money was recovered and went back to the company. The necklace was never reported to be stolen so Cindy was allowed to keep it."

'No harm done,' she thought to herself. 'They got all their money back.' And the gift he gave her was turned into a fortune for herself. But that gift was not as precious as the gift of life he gave her.

THE CURSE OF ANGELO

Who would ever think that Tommy Burke, washed up ace private detective, would end up in the same jail cell as a hit man of the East Side mob, Tony Romano.

It was surely a coincidence, it would seem, unless the police chief was hoping they would eliminate each other. Burke and Romano hated each other, having traded bullets for a number of years. Romano even had a scar to prove the point. It's a miracle that either one survived the years of bloody mob violence.

But there they were, roomies in cell 14 in the metropolitan jail with all the five star accommodations, including a sink, a toilet, two cots, two chairs, a wobbly table, and a cracked mirror. A bashful 40 watt bulb worked overtime standing guard over the two derelicts.

Romano was asleep when Burke entered the cell and didn't wake up until Tommy had stirred around a while. Then Tony spoke as he raised his head. "Do my eyes deceive me or is that Tommy Burke I see through these blood shot, blurry eyes of mine?"

"It's me, all right," Burke responded with a less than enthusiastic retort of exasperation.

"Well what are you doing here?" Romano asked and laughed. "Did you come to bail me out?"

"I was just going to ask you the same question."

Romano rolled over in his cot, put his feet on the floor, sat up, and continued. "I'm under suspicion for some petty crime of murder over on 18th Street. I'll be out of here in a little while when they check out my story. And you?"

Burke paced across the floor and laughed. "Petty crime of murder?

That's just like you, Tony. Always laughing in the face of adversity. As for me, I'll be out of here in two shakes. I'm being held on suspicion, too. They think I beat up some guy on the north side. I have an alibi and I'll be out of here quick as a wink."

"Lucky for both of us, I'd say." Romano answered as he yawned from his nap. "Why do you suppose they put us in the same cell? We've been trying to kill each other for years."

"Beats me," Burke stated. "I guess it was Chief Simpson's idea of a joke. Or maybe they didn't have any more room. The jail is pretty full right now."

Romano laid back down on the cot with his head propped up against the wall and watched a fly buzzing around the ceiling. His black hair was showing signs of aging with a few streaks of gray. A few stress wrinkles went across his face making a symmetrical pattern.

"I'm sure your boss, Angelo Prunetti, will be picking you up soon. Or maybe one of his cronies."

"I don't think so," Romano answered. "I'm no longer part of the so-called family."

Burke stopped pacing and looked at Tony. "What do you mean by that?"

"He let me go. Happened this morning. He said I was no longer needed and for me to hit the road."

"Uh oh," Tommy answered. "You're in big trouble."

"How do you figure that?"

"The mob doesn't just let you go. He's setting you up for a hit."

"You're crazy, Burke. I was a loyal member. He wouldn't do that."

"Use your head, Romano. How many times have you seen it happen. One of these days the cops are going to pin some murder on you and it's either tell everything you know or you spend the rest of your life in jail-or maybe worse. If you do tell everything you know, the mob will go down the toilet and so will Prunetti. And you will get off easy. So they bump you off to protect themselves."

"Yeah," responded Tony. "You may be right but what can I do about it?"

"Nothing. You're a dead man."

"I didn't think you'd be very sympathetic, Tommy. Maybe you could help me out," Tony asked in a sarcastic way.

"I don't have any pull around here any more, Tony. I'm finished as a private detective in this city. They pulled my license and banned me from ever doing detective work again."

"Wow!! Why did they do that?"

"I had to take some bribes to solve some of the cases. Maybe I was above the law once in a while but I got the job done. And this is the thanks I get for helping out the city."

"My heart bleeds for you," Tony said with a laugh. "At least you don't have Angelo Prunetti stalking you."

"Yeah, I guess I'm blessed in a way but I'm leaving town."

"I can't leave," Tony stated. "I got nowhere to go. So I'll just have to try to hide out in my apartment and stay hid in the shadows somehow."

The two jailbirds exchanged stories for a while until the cell opened up. The jailor looked at Tommy and said, "You're free to go, Burke. But the chief said he wants you out of town by sundown."

"See you around, Tony." Tommy said as he left the cell.

Just then he stopped in his tracks and looked back at Romano. "You can't go back to your apartment. I'm sure they are waiting for you there. I'll meet you in the lobby and we'll talk some more."

"Sure thing, Tommy."

Mystified by this, Tony waited in cell 14 for another hour. He was finally released after the charges were dropped and the chief said he was free to go- for now but not to leave town. He met Tommy in the waiting room and they walked outside in the street. It was nice to be free and they both breathed in the fresh air as they soaked in the sunshine.

"You're going back to my apartment, Tony. You can stay there till I figure something out."

"Are you crazy," Romano responded. "We're supposed to be enemies. Are you going to finally finish me off and deprive Prunetti the pleasure of doing it? You certainly tried enough times."

"No, of course not. But I feel sorry for you in a way. I just want to help. There's no reason for us to be enemies anymore. We're both washed up."

They got into Tommy's car and sped off down the street. In a few minutes, they were in front of Burke's apartment complex.

"So this is where you live," Tony stated as he scanned the building.

"Yeah, this is home. At least temporarily," Tommy answered.

They went inside and took the stairs up to the third floor. They entered room 312.

"I still don't get it," Romano barked. "Why are you wanting to help me?"

"Why not. You got no friends. I got no friends. We're no longer enemies, are we? Besides, I have a plan."

"I can't wait to hear this."

Tommy went to the refrigerator and brought out a couple of beers and they sat at the kitchen table.

"I'm not so sure about this, Burke." Romano said as he popped the top of the beer can. "I mean I appreciate your interest in me but you're putting yourself at a tremendous risk."

"So what," quipped Burke. "We've lived with risks most of our adult lives. Might as well continue with it for a while longer."

"Here's the plan," Tommy stated as he took a big gulp of beer. "I have this friend out west and he owns a ranch. Nobody knows him here and I'm sure he'd give us a job out there. You can change your name and we'll work as cowhands."

"You got to be kidding," Tony said with a laugh and a burp. "What do you and I know about working on a ranch? And where is this place?"

"Wyoming. Nothing but wide-open spaces, clean air, and nature."

"I don't know, Tommy. I'll have to think about it."

Just then someone knocked on the door. "Tony, go hide in the closet till I get rid of whoever it is."

Tony grabbed a .38 revolver and scurried into the hall closet and shut the door. Tommy looked through the peep hole on the front door, grabbed a revolver of his own and hid it behind his back. He didn't recognize two tough looking gentlemen but carefully opened the door.

"Yes, what can I do for you?"

"We're looking for Tony Romano. A man that fit his description was seen going into this apartment house. Thought you might have seen him."

"And who are you?"

"Never mind who we are. Just tell us if you've seen him." The two tough guys gazed inside the apartment but failed to notice two beer cans on the table.

"Haven't seen anybody," answered Burke sharply. He opened the door wider.

"See, there's nobody here but me," answered Tommy with coolness. He could see that the two men were not convinced.

"I do believe you must be Tommy Burke," one of the men said with a bit of sarcasm in his voice. "You wouldn't be hiding Romano in this apartment, would you?"

"What a joke that is," answered Burke with a chuckle. "We tried to kill each other a dozen times. Why would I want that scum bag in my apartment? I hope you get him."

"Just the same, we're keeping an eye on this place. And if you're hiding him, you are both going to pay dearly. And you know the cops aren't going to lift a finger to help you."

"Yeah, but just don't get in my way," Tommy stated as he stared at the two guys.

They left, and Tommy closed the door. "You can come out now, Tony."

Romano emerged cautiously and stated, "I changed my mind. I think I'm going to like Wyoming. Those two guys were Archie DeLasco and Bennie Milano, two of Prunetti's hit men."

"I thought so. We gotta get out of here and fast," decried Burke.

"So," answered Romano, "we just going to walk out the front door while Prunetti's men gun us down?"

"No, I got a plan."

"You didn't have to call me a 'scum bag,'" Tony said with a bit of sarcasm and a grin.

For the next five days, the two derelicts played it cool and didn't venture out except for Tommy to get groceries. Tony stayed under wraps and didn't even go near the window. Tommy's plan was to sneak out Tony in broad daylight dressed like a woman.

"You've got to be kidding," Tony quipped. "I think I'd rather be gunned down."

The plan was put into action as Tommy measured Tony and went to a dress shop and gave the dimensions to the dressmaker for three dresses and three wigs. In a few days, the dresses were finished, and Tommy also bought some lipstick and some high heel shoes. He took it back to his apartment, piece by piece, in a briefcase. It took several trips because he knew he was being watched. He could feel the eyes on him as he entered the apartment doorway but did not act like he knew.

Tony was not very happy with the procedure but knew it was necessary to maintain anonymity with the disguises. "I really appreciate all the trouble to get me out of here," Tony said as he guzzled a beer and munched on cheese crackers. "You really think this cowboy deal will work?"

"It will if we ever get out of here," Tommy said. "Just be patient."

The two developed a cautious friendship, still under the influence of a bit of suspicion that built up for years past. However, Tony realized the Tommy had saved him from death by the two thugs that came to the door. And death sometimes doesn't come easy for a marked man hunted by the mob. His confidence in Tommy was growing.

By the seventh day, they were ready to leave the apartment. Tommy would leave first and drive a couple blocks to a shopping center. It was planned with the precision of a top-level CIA operation. Every move had to be carefully calculated and executed because they knew that Prunetti was already suspecting that Tony Romano was hiding in the apartment house and had his thugs casing the building and watching their every move.

Tommy waited until Mrs. Johnson, a widow woman, was wanting to go shopping. She was wearing a blue dress and had gray hair and Tommy offered to drive her there. She agreed, and they left the apartment at 8:05 AM with some of Prunetti's thugs following in a black sedan.

Tony, with the wardrobe provided by Tommy, dressed in a red dress and a black wig. He had a large purse, put on lipstick and wore stockings. He wore high heels which gave Tony some trouble at first but after a lot of practice in the apartment, he was walking pretty well.

A couple more of Prunetti's thugs were watching from across the street as Tony left the apartment at 8:31 AM in a taxi to a dentist office, three blocks away from the shopping center. Archie and Benny, Prunetti's thugs were watching all the time and were suspicious. They decided to follow Tony's taxi. Prunetti was getting impatient and wanted results.

Sometimes called the "Curse of Angelo," a marked man was certain to either die from multiple gunshot wounds in an alley or simply disappear without a trace.

Meanwhile, Tommy and Mrs. Johnson arrived at the shopping center and at 8:20 AM and both got out and went inside.

Tony arrived at the dentist office at 8:40 AM and went inside where he immediately went into the ladies restroom and changed into a green dress and a brown wig, then called another taxi. This time it took him to the shopping center where Tommy had gone and was waiting inside at the sporting goods department.

Prunetti's thugs waited in front of the dentist office but the 'lady' they saw go inside never came back out.

Tony went in the store, changed into a blue dress in the ladies room and a gray wig, looking as much like Mrs. Johnson as he could. He then met up with Tommy and they proceeded out to the car. Prunetti's men were watching but did not suspect anything, for they thought Tommy was taking Mrs. Johnson back to her apartment.

They drove off, nonchalantly down South Boulevard toward the expressway. "I think we did it," Tommy said with confidence. Tony was not going to change clothes until they were sure they weren't being followed. After about twenty miles, they were heading down Route 49 and out into the country.

"I think you can change now," Tommy said as Tony was glad to get out of the women's clothes and into his regular attire.

"I don't see how women wear those blasted high heels," Tony said as he wiped off the lipstick and took off the wig.

They travelled all afternoon and most of the night until they stopped at a motel for a short rest. The next morning, they instinctively looked around before leaving to see if they had been followed. Tony ditched his women's clothes.

"The coast is clear," Tommy said. They continued for a couple of days until they finally reached the ranch. "You have to change your name, Tony, and never use your real name again."

"I understand," Tony answered. "How 'bout Blackjack Maynard?" Tony said with a laugh.

"Sounds fine to me," Tommy answered.

They pulled up to the ranch house where he was greeted by his friend, Buck Allen. Tommy went in and left Tony outside while he told Buck what he had in mind.

Meanwhile, Tony looked around outside and thought it was the most beautiful country he'd ever seen. The sky was bluer than he'd ever seen, and the mountains loomed beautifully in the distance. The sound of cattle could be heard in the distance while he saw cowboys milling around the bunk house.

Tommy emerged from the house with Buck and he got acquainted with Tony. "Tommy explained everything," Buck said as he shook Tony's hand. "Tommy and I go back a long way. He saved my life once and I owe him everything. Any friend of Tommy's is a friend of mine. I hope you like it here. We're break you in slowly and you will gradually get the hang of things around here. We are a cattle ranch and there's lots of work to do. You'll be living in the bunkhouse with the other cowboys. I've got a new set of clothes for both of you."

As the days passed, Tommy and Tony started to fit in just fine. Tony and Tommy began to look like real cowboys. They lived in the bunkhouse, sometimes slept out under the stars and next to a campfire when they rode the range. As Blackjack Maynard, his new identity was never questioned, for some of the other cowboys had questionable pasts, too. Nobody asked any questions.

In the Sunday newspaper a few months later was an article about the Prunetti gang. It read, "Angelo Prunetti and his thugs convicted for tax evasion and murder."

"Do you think we are home free?" Tony asked Tommy one evening after a hard day herding cattle.

"No doubt about it, Blackjack ol' pal. Prunetti is finished once and for all. And we're living the best life there is."

"And we broke the Curse of Angelo," Tony said with a laugh as he looked up at the stars.

SHARKEY AND THE BLIPS

Thomas Adams and his cousin Mary Caroline had always kept the secret of the Blips to themselves for the protection of those tiny human-like creatures who lived beneath the ground under the big oak tree. They were only six inches tall and vulnerable to all sorts of dangers. These included hungry cats and foxes, owls and hawks, snakes, and other predators. But humans were their biggest fear. It was common knowledge that human's love of money would encourage their capture. The Blips would bring incredible monetary returns as well as notoriety to the owner, not to mention eventually digging up their world for the rest of the world to see.

It was, therefore, paramount that the secret of the Blips be kept under wraps.

Thomas was the first human to discover the Blips when he was walking through the woods one bright summer day. He accidentally saw one that was cornered by a hungry cat. Rescuing the Blip named Scuffy, they became friends. Thomas was then invited by their leader, Bebob, to enter the sacred entrance and see their world. He asked Bebob if his cousin Mary Caroline could see them too and Bebob agreed to a visit, as long as they vowed to keep it a secret.

A magic dust was provided which reduced Thomas and Mary Caroline to the size of the Blips and another dust would reverse the process later and would return them to their original size.

Then they were able to explore the magical world with the friendly creatures beneath the ground, led by their leader, Bebob. and his friendly female assistant, Pinky. The Blip's world spanned a large area with a banquet hall, farms for growing mushrooms, storage areas for fruits and vegetables, and the most impressive of all, a town deep underground where numerous houses and streets went deep below the surface of the forest. It was illuminated by glowing phosphorescent street lamps. The Blips worked and played and kept their world clean and safe from humans and other intruders. Blinker was the door guard that stood watch at the entrance, which was a small door at the base of a big oak tree.

Several years ago, Thomas and Mary Caroline were summoned by Bebob when Skipper and Cricket got lost in the woods when they ventured too far from their tree on a berry gathering trip. It was a harrowing experience for the two tiny Blips as they barely escaped all sorts of dangers including a hawk, a cat, a snake, and a hungry rat.

None of these experiences were more scary than being chased by two humans, intent on capturing the two small creatures and putting them on permanent display for the world to see, perhaps in a carnival.

By finding a toy boat along the side of a creek, Skipper and Cricket were able to escape as they rode the rapids down a creek.

Thomas and Mary Caroline were in hot pursuit as they tracked the lost Blips along paths and through the forest. They finally spotted them drifting helplessly down the creek and rushed on ahead.

When it looked like the two Blips were going to perish as they went over a waterfall, Thomas was there with a net to catch them. He and Mary Caroline returned them safely back to their home and they all celebrated with a party in the Blip's banquet hall.

A few years before Mary Caroline was introduced to the Blips, she was fortunate to meet Sharkey LeGrand, space explorer and former space pirate. Sharkey's spaceship, the Dragon, landed in a nearby field late one night when everyone else was asleep to take on Nitrogen to replenish their power system.

She and her sister Elizabeth went outside to see the spaceship and met Sharkey LeGrand, Bobo Whalebone, Stretch McGirt, and Wilma Lurking, the crew of the ship.

Mary Caroline and Elizabeth got to ride the Dragon to a faraway, man made planet called Skytropolis, where they were treated to a tour, authorized by Sharkey's boss, Inspector Locknose of the intergalactic space patrol.

After they saw many wondrous things on this incredible planet, Sharkey and his crew returned them safely back to their home. He said someday they would return to earth for another visit. Mary Caroline and Elizabeth kept this secret for they knew no one would ever believe such a bizarre story.

It was on a bright, summer day that Thomas and Mary Caroline went into the woods looking for blackberries. They ventured down the trail, beside the pasture, along the creek and over the hill. They walked through the pine thicket, then between the ferns and flowers as the neared the big oak tree beside a meadow of beautiful yellow flowers. But they sensed something was not right. It was quiet, too quiet, and none of the small trails that the Blips used for searching for food had been traveled on for quite some time. Some grass had even started to grow up on some of the trails. Something must be wrong, they thought.

When they got to the big oak tree they knelt down and knocked on the tiny door expecting to see Blinker, the door guard, holding his little wooden spear. Nothing happened. They waited a couple of minutes.

"I'm worried," Mary Caroline said as she looked closer at the door.

"I hope nothing has happened to the Blips," Thomas said as he knocked again. Still no answer.

"Do we still have some of that magic dust?" Mary Carolina inquired as she looked at Thomas.

"Yes," Thomas answered. "I'll go back and get some and we'll go inside and take a look.

Thomas ran back to the house and brought the two kinds of magic dust. They sprinkled each other and suddenly they reduced down to a mere six inches. They stood at the entrance and managed to push open the door. They peered inside. It was quiet with no Blinker. The phosphorescent lamps still illuminated the tunnel that led to the banquet hall. They followed it and still no sign of anyone. However, Mary Caroline noticed a hand written note attacked to a root hanging from the ceiling.

It read, "To Thomas and Mary Caroline. We knew you'd come looking for us. We're in real danger. Follow the directions to our new location." It was signed, Bebob.

Thomas and Mary Caroline went deeper into the cavernous home of the Blips and it was deserted. The town that lay deep underground was abandoned. Still the street lights illuminated the houses and paths along the myriad of homes. No sign of life anywhere. Even the storage areas were empty.

"Let's get out of here," Mary Caroline said with a bit of panic in her voice.

"I'm with you," Thomas answered as they backtracked along the corridor to the entrance. When they were outside, they sprinkled themselves with the other dust and immediately became their normal size.

They followed the directions that took them deep into the woods. After travelling about a hundred yards, they looked for a large rock that Bebob mentioned in his note. To the right of the rock was a thick briar patch that would have been impossible for Thomas and Mary Caroline to go through. As they stood there, they heard a voice from beneath them.

"I'm glad you came, I knew you would." It was Bebob along with Pinky and they looked worried. Thomas gently picked up Bebob and Pinky and held them in his hand.

"We had to leave," Bebob said. "We overheard voices outside and they are going to cut down the big oak tree, dig up this whole area, and put in a housing development."

"That's terrible," Mary Caroline said with deep concern.

"We had to leave or be destroyed," Pinky replied. "I think we'll be pretty safe here for a while until we can find a new place to go. And I'm not sure we have that much time."

"I heard the same thing about the housing development but I didn't think they would really do it," Thomas stated with dismay.

"The plans are already in the works," Bebob said. "They are going to start any time now."

"I noticed some earth moving equipment nearby but I didn't know they were really going to cut down the oak tree," Thomas added. "Is there anything we can do?"

"Nothing that we know of," Pinky said. "I think we're pretty safe here for a while but we have to leave this area."

"We'll go back home," Mary Caroline said, "and we'll check on you in a couple of days. Maybe we can help you move to a safe area."

Meanwhile, Thomas and Mary Caroline went home, extremely worried and distraught that the Blips were forced to leave their home. And as for the housing project, this was "progress," they were told by their parents. A lot of people were going to make a lot of money developing that property.

That night that Mary Caroline tried to sleep but couldn't. She was so worried. Then, at precisely 2:00 AM, she was awakened by a strange light below her house in the field. It briefly illuminated her room then died away. She got up out of her bed and peered out the window. A strange silver spaceship was sitting in the field. "It's Sharkey and his crew!" she said with excitement. "They've come back. I bet they can help."

Being careful not to wake her parents, she crept outside and greeted Sharkey, the inter-galactic explorer and space patrol officer. "Getting more Nitrogen, Sharkey?" she asked politely.

"Yes," Sharkey responded. "It's good to see you again. I hope you don't mind us using your field as a temporary parking space. We'll be out of here in a few minutes. How have you been?"

"I'm doing well," Mary Caroline answered. "Take all the time you want."

She was then greeted by Bobo, Stretch, and Wilma, the crew of Sharkey's spaceship, the Dragon, who came out to see her. She then had an idea. Looking at Sharkey, she inquired." Maybe you can help out the Blips."

"What are Blips?" Sharkey asked with interest.

"They are small human like creatures that live in the forest."

Sharkey looked at his crew somewhat puzzled. "Are you sure you haven't been dreaming?"

"It's true. Just come with me and I'll show you. I know it's late and dark but can you come with Thomas and me now?"

"Anything to help out a friend," Sharkey said. "Any friend of yours is a friend of ours."

Thomas was spending the night at Mary Caroline's house and she rushed back and woke him. She explained that her space visitors were outside in the field.

Thomas had heard about Sharkey LeGrand but never thought he'd meet him in person. He was so excited. Mary Caroline had told Thomas about her trip to Skytropolis and how they had promised to return someday.

They all walked to the area of the Blip's new home. Thomas called for Bebob and he emerged from the thicket under the bright full moon with Pinky and was greeted by Mary Caroline who picked him up and showed them to Sharkey and his crew.

Bebob explained to Sharkey the predicament they were in.

"I think we have a solution to your problem, Bebob," Sharkey announced. "You can come back with us to Skytropolis and live on my farm."

"What a great idea," Mary Caroline said with great enthusiasm. "I can go with you and show you around."

Bebob went back into the thicket and met with all the other Blips and it was agreed that it would be a good idea to at least try it.

"I promise you will be safe and no harm will come to you," Sharkey said. "You can start a new underground city just like the old one."

"You can trust them," Mary Caroline assured the Blips as they gathered around.

In a few minutes, all the Blips had emerged from the briars and were ready to embark on their journey.

"We'll take them to Skytropolis and later we'll be back and take you to visit them," Sharkey promised. "Give us a week or so to get them settled."

The Blips boarded the Dragon and off they went after a tearful goodbye to Thomas and Mary Caroline.

"Don't worry," Thomas said to Bebob. "We're going to see you soon."

The Dragon soared off into space with their precious cargo as they headed for Skytropolis, the city in the sky and a new home for the Blips.

The adults had their way and eventually the housing development was built. Thankfully, the big oak tree was left standing for aesthetic purposes as houses and driveways would be built around it.

The tiny door at the base of the tree was carefully sealed up and concealed by Thomas and Mary Caroline and no one ever suspected that the tiny Blips ever existed. Beneath the big tree was the remnants of a fantastic secret, never to be revealed.

Thomas and Mary Caroline patiently waited for Sharkey's return for they knew that they would eventually come back to Earth and take them back to Skytropolis to see the Blips.

THE GHOST OF CAMP DANIEL BOONE

There are ghost stories that are fiction and there are ghost stories that are true. This is a true story about a ghost that I encountered when I was eleven years old. I affirm here and now that I am telling the truth when I write about a ghostly encounter and other strange happenings in August of 1960.

A long time ago but firmly entrenched in my memory was that fantastic trip to Boy Scout camp in the mountains of western North Carolina called Camp Daniel Boone. It's still there and still operational and serves both boy and girl scouts, along with weddings and other events. It's vibrant part of the community and isolated enough to be in the wilderness. After all, what good is a boy scout in the middle of a city. He'd much rather be out in the wilderness with his buddies and nature.

When we arrived on that Sunday afternoon we went to an orientation at a place called Chip's Chapel. It was named for a boy scout that tragically died some time before that; not at the camp but somewhere else. The chapel is still there and is in a beautiful location, overlooking the lake. It's used for weddings and other events and still serves as the opening ceremony site for scouts two have arrived, preparing them for a week of fun and adventure.

Camp Daniel Boone was a great place to be when I was there in August of 1960. The ladies in the cafeteria, or actually the mess hall as they called it, fixed superb meals and we thoroughly enjoyed them, Boys romping through the woods, swimming and canoeing, hiking and working up a big appetite were always hungry. The nice ladies were always quick to supply us with great nutritional meals and lots of it.

Our scoutmaster was a veteran of World War II. His name was Leonard Wells and he had been in the 82nd Airborne and jumped during the war. He'd seen combat but wouldn't talk about it to us. I felt safe around him as he was big and strong and knew how to handle any situation.

Our assistant scoutmaster was also in the war. He was a retired master sergeant with thirty years in the Army. He had been in numerous theaters of war and had seen plenty of combat. We called him Sarge Matthews, which is what he preferred to be called. Sarge was rough and tough and I also felt safe around him. He used to like to read old western novels like Louis L'Amour and Zane Grey. He kept a good supply of those paperback books in his tent, which was right beside mine.

During that week at Camp Daniel Boone we lived in canvas tents that were made for two people and set up off the ground. I assume it helped keep out the snakes. They were open ended on both the front and back. I can still smell the tent canvas in my mind. We all had army cots to sleep on and it was perfect for us as that was all part of the adventure. My tent mate was a second cousin of mine, Tommy Bramlett. My brother, John, who was also a scout and a bit older, had a tent mate named Charles Matthews, the son of our own Sarge Matthews.

My first experience with the supernatural came one sunny afternoon when a few of us fellows were talking outside the tents. I was about fifty feet away from my tent and I could see the front very well. I suddenly looked up and saw someone enter my tent. I even saw the tent flap move. I was the only one who saw this. I ran up to my tent, thinking that someone was wanting to steal something. Not that I had any money or valuables, but maybe he was trying to look for something valuable. I went inside my tent and saw nothing. I ran out the back and saw nothing. No sign of anyone being inside or outside the tent. Nobody running away. I dismissed it but thought it a bit strange.

That evening I saw someone go into the bath house, which was just below our tents. I never saw him before and I wandered down to investigate. There was no one inside. This was strange happening number two.

That night was the weirdest of all. I lay down to go to sleep as Tommy was already asleep. I closed my eyes and opened them and the whole night had passed in the blink of an eye-literally. I had not moved and did not feel like I'd been asleep. The next think I knew was Sarge going from tent to tent saying in his familiar gruff voice, "Rise and shine, time to get up."

I can't explain this but it happened one more time while I was at Camp Daniel Boone. Another night that went in the blink of an eye. It never happened again since that time and I never had any hallucinations that I know of. I was not on drugs because we didn't even know what drugs were back then.

To this day, I truly believe that I saw a ghost and experienced his presence. Could that have been Chip that I saw? Could I have been in Chip's tent that week? We will never know. I have inquired several times about ghost sightings there and none seem to have happened. No one knows about any ghost sightings there.

Printed in the United States
By Bookmasters